T0196275

1865

Cojacker Verdi

AuthorHouse™
1663 Liberty Drive
Bloomington, IN 47403
www.authorhouse.com
Phone: 1-800-839-8640

Published by AuthorHouse 12/20/2011

ISBN: 978-1-4685-2867-1 (sc)
ISBN: 978-1-4685-2866-4 (e)

This book is printed on acid-free paper.

ONE

IN THE YEAR 1865 the Old West was still young. If you know history you should know that the Old West lasted half a century. The Civil War ended in 1865 and people thought everything was getting back to normal with their lives, with no further worries. Little did they know that their troubles were yet to begin again.

In the same year, Abraham Lincoln was assassinated because some people didn't like what he had done when he was president of the United States. Word spread quickly, and everybody got the biggest surprise of their lives, that their most powerful and respected leader had died. Abraham Lincoln will be always be beloved and will be down in history as one of the greatest leaders in America.

In 1865, people are going west to start new lives.

They are also taking their families so they don't leave anything behind. Slowly people are naming their new land after their own or different names with their own different meanings. So far this has been a hard year for everybody in the Old West, like before the Civil War ended and Abraham Lincoln was assassinated.

Our story begins in the center of Texas where most cowboys hang out, having the time of their lives. Fort Worth, Texas, isn't a big city yet, but the story starts outside of the town of Forth Worth. Outside Forth Worth, Texas is mostly a farming area. People are friendly and down to earth, always being there to help those who need help.

In the center of the farms in Fort Worth, Texas, there is a family by the name of Hahn. They're a normal kind of family without any troubles or enemies inside or outside of Texas. John has been married to his wife, Sharon, for more than twenty years, and they have had three children together, all hardworking boys in their adulthood.

The oldest, Derek, is six feet-almost as tall as his father with thin to medium build like his father. Little does Derek know that this will be the year of adventure of 1865. In the Old West Derek had heard about lots of adventures in his life before the century is over or before he dies, whichever comes first.

On a normal Sunday afternoon, the Han family goes to their wagon to go home from church, minding their own business without any worries. Then suddenly Derek wants to say something to his father-something that he has been meaning to say for a very long time, but has been scared to ask his own father. But at the same time, he thinks to himself that it never hurts to.

"Dad, I been meaning to ask you this for a very long time but was afraid to ask you," said Derek.

"Ask me. You know that I'm an open-minded person," said John.

"Here goes. Dad, when you were much younger than me, like a child, did you ever dream of doing something besides farming?" said Derek.

"No, so far farming has always been inside my blood, just like my father and his father so on. Why?" asked John.

"Just a thought. I always thought that there is something more than farming, that there was a big world out there waiting to be explored or have adventures in their lives," said Derek.

"All right all right, stop and think about this before you make any decisions. It never hurts to stop and think in life. And let me know by tonight," said John.

"You really mean it, dad? I could?" said Derek.

"Of course I mean it. But let me know by tonight so you have enough time to think this throw," said John.

"All right, I'll let you know," said Derek.

Derek understood why his father wanted to know by tonight, because Derek will have enough time to think this throw before he does something that he's going to regret in the end. Right now, it's three in the afternoon, so he has until tonight to give his own father an answer. So far Derek has been very lucky that he has an understanding father on these kinds of things.

It's eight in the evening. After five long hours Derek had enough hours to think about it, and Derek decided to leave his own home to have adventure in his life. So the best things to do was to tell his parents. Derek's father is sitting in his chair in the main room near the fireplace. He looked like he was waiting for Derek's answer. He looked back and saw Derek.

Right away John knows from the look on Derek's face that he wanted to leave the farm, so John is willing to help him in any way he can. Derek is very happy that his father understood his feelings about it, and glad that he's willing to help him in any way he can. So right away tonight they got his stuff ready for the big day tomorrow when he leaves.

Sharon promises herself not to cry, but she can't. She loves Derek and took care of him for so many years, and the hardest thing is saying good-bye to her own son. Morning came, and everybody is outside waiting for their chance to say good-bye to Derek. It's best for the family not to tell the other farms, except if they bring it up, because they don't want to feel sad about this.

"Good-bye, my son. Don't forget to write to us as much as you can," said Sharon.

"Don't worry, Mom. I won't forget," said Derek.

"You listen to your mother and be careful on who you trust, Derek. There are a lot of weird people out there taking advantage of good people like us," said John.

"Don't worry, Dad. I'll be careful," said Derek.

Derek hugs his other brothers and said good-bye to them. So far it's a very hard thing to do to say good-bye to loved ones, but he's glad that none of the other farms are here to say good-bye, because Derek doesn't want to say good-bye. In less than a second, Derek got onto his black horse and took off. So far Sharon cried pretty hard. She promised herself not to, but she broke that promise to herself. Sharon can't believe that her own baby is gone, kind of like a bird leaving the nest.

Derek took off, following the sun without any trouble. He can't wait to see what's across the mountain, to see what's behind the shadows, to see what will happen to him. At the same time Derek will be ready for anything that comes to him and knows how to deal with it without any trouble. First things first. Derek needs a gun to protect himself and for anything that will pop out. The last thing Derek needs is the surprise of a gun pointed right in front of him.

The best place to get a good fighting arm is in Dallas, right here in Texas. Derek is very lucky that the saved enough money to buy a very powerful gun. That's the first place that Derek will go, first to buy a very powerful gun and also a chance to go to Dallas, some strange things about the part of Texas. He's hoping that some of the strange things that he heard aren't true.

Two weeks passed. Derek finally made it to Dallas without any trouble so far. Derek traveled day and night; that's how he managed to travel east. Dallas is a nice, normal, average city, with not a care in the world. People mind their own business, with not a care in the world. The first thing that Derek said was, "What a city!"

The first place he went was to the gun store to buy the most powerful handgun that money could buy, praying that the gun store owner won't give him a hard time because he's new at this. The gun store is at the center of town, next door to the sheriff's office so no one will give the gun store a hard time.

Derek tied his horse outside near the sheriff's office so no one will take the horse. He calmly went inside the gun store without any worries. The gun store clerk is ready for anything that pops out, and he even has a gun ready in case anything happens. The last thing that the gun store owner wants is a surprise. The clerk looks like he ahs been robed a few times in the past, so if the could just talk he has nothing to worry about. And Derek will never steal from anybody.

"May I help you with anything, sir?" said the clerk.

"Yeah, what's the most powerful gun you have? Money is no object to me, and believe me, you got nothing to worry about. You don't have to call me sir just good old Derek," said Derek.

"All right. I'm Larry, and you act like a nice person. I'm sorry for how I'm acting. It's just that I have been robbed a few times, and right now I really need a break," said Larry.

"Don't worry. I'm not going to hurt you. I'm new here. I just need a gun," said Derek.

"Why? I'm hoping you don't mind me asking," said Larry.

"I can't say. It's personal, and I could understand your worries about this," said Derek.

"I understand. You got nothing to worry about. I'll show you everything," said Larry.

Larry showed him every powerful gun he had. The Peacemaker gun was enough to take down anybody and the most beautiful color of black. Derek saw the highest-priced gun so far, and it's something he will buy. The reason is because there had to be some magic in the gun when Derek looked at it, and somehow that gun and he will work together like no other.

The cost of that gun is twenty-five dollars. It's a lot of money, but it will be worth it because nobody's going to mess with him. Derek paid for the gun without any trouble and also the bullets that come with it. So far Derek got a good deal with it and left the city without any worries.

The sun is coming down, and like before, Derek followed the sun to see what will come to him. But Derek will be ready for anything, and he means anything. At the same time Derek needs a new nickname, and from now on he will be called D.H., so no one will know his background and so no one will ever hurt his family. He'll be mysterious no matter what.

TWO

D.H TRAVELED AS far east as he could and made it to a city named-well, D.H. doesn't know yet, but sooner or later he'll find out. First things first. Get something to drink, but the first thing that D.H thought to himself was that the city looked a ghost town, something that D.H. had never seen before.

The reason why D.H thought of that was that there were only a few people outside making some trade, but everybody else was inside for some reason-like everybody had something to hide. The second thought to himself was that this town looked like a great place to start an adventure, but that he needed to find a place to stay for a little bit until he got to the bottom of things.

D.H. had a long trip to far east, and he really needed something to drink. The first place that he saw to get something to drink was a bar a little bit down the street, so D.H. helped himself. As he rode his horse down the street a little bit, some of the people looked at him in a different way, but not in a way that most people expected. They all looked a D.H. like they were afraid of him for some reason, which D.H. didn't know.

He tied his horse outside and calmly went inside the bar, but before he could go inside D.H. got a deep breath and got prepared for anything that might pop out, that might be thrown at him. That's the last thing that D.H. wants, but he is ready for anything that comes to him, even in a strange new place. A second later D.H. went inside the bar without any trouble. The second when D.H. came inside, everybody looked at D.H. in a weird way, like they'd never seen an outside before.

D.H. didn't care as long as he could go up to the bar to get something to drink. So far D.H. has never seen so many people before acting like they all have something to hide. The best thing to do was to sit at the end of the bar. After a minute or two everything got back to normal and everybody was doing their own business; D.H. is minding his own business. The bartender came up to him to help him.

"Good afternoon. I'm Travis. I've never seen you around here before. Are you new here at Cold Creek?," asked Travis.

"Petty much. I'm D.H., and it's nice to meet you Travis. There any good hotels to stay at here?" said D.H.

"There is one good place here in this town, but I

should warn you about this town. This isn't a good place to stay. There are a lot of outlaws that raise havoc around here. So I think it's best to leave before you get yourself killed," said Travis.

"Thanks for the warning, but I think you guys need somebody to help you guys. I'm more like a guardian angel you guys need," said D.H.

"Yeah, right. That's what the last guy said before he got his head cut off, if you know what I mean," said Travis.

"I know what you mean, but I'm here to help. There was a reason why I traveled east, and that's why I'm here now. If you don't mind, tell me where the hotel is," said D.H.

"All right, I'll tell you where the hotel is, but I'm not coming to your funeral when you get yourself killed," said Travis.

"I'll take that chance," said D.H.

The bartender gave the directions to the hotel at the end of town, and D.H. left the bar. So far the bartender decided to pray for him that this one wouldn't get killed and try to help everybody here in Cold Creek. D.H. was trying to find out why the town was called Cold Creek, but sooner or later D.H. will know.

D.H got settled into his room, and the first thing was to write back home to his family telling them that he's all right, and that he made it to a town in the far east. It's best not to tell them it's a very dangerous town, because he doesn't want to worry them too much about him; that he's all right. At the same time D.H. is wondering how his parents will take it if they find out what's happening, but he stops to think that it's best not to tell them, for their own safety.

He finished the letter and made sure that his parents wouldn't worry about him too much. It was pretty late, so he decided to go to bed and mail it tomorrow; it's the best time to do it. D.H. is trying his best to go to sleep, but he keeps on hearing something outside. So he decides to go and investigate and at the same time make sure that they won't notice him.

Mostly they are talking outside. D.H. is on the second floor downstairs in a restaurant, but they are talking from outside the restaurant, so it's best to hear them through the window. He calmly opens the window and hears three men talking. And there is something, all right-something that D.H. has been waiting for. Right away D.H. knows that they are gangsters from the way they are dressed.

"I heard what's going to happen tomorrow night here in Cold Creek. Is it true?" said the first gangster.

"Yeah, it's true that there will be a shooting here in this town. So far we are putting the whole town in hostage if everybody wont give us the money tomorrow at high noon," said the second gangster.

"We will have more than enough to live on for a very long time without any worries," said the third gangster.

"So the two of you know what we're going to do tomorrow night?" said the first gangster.

"Yeah, we know, so you got nothing to worry about," said the third gangster.

"All right, that's good. I'll see the both of you tomorrow at high noon, and you two know what to do," said the first gangster.

"Yeah, see you tomorrow," said the third gangster.

"Same here," said the second gangster.

The three of them left the area, but first they made sure that no one was watching them. The second they finished their private meeting, D.H. went inside so they wouldn't see him and know that somebody was on to them. All three of them didn't see anybody, and they left in a hurry. So tomorrow D.H. has his work cut out for him what's going to happen, and he's willing to defend everybody here in Cold Creek.

Morning came, and the post office opened. D.H. mailed his letter and went back to his room at the hotel and started to think what he should do to scare those outlaws. If it's a war they want, it's a war they will get. Suddenly it came out of nowhere to his mind that D.H. will shoot to scare them away and he'll hide somewhere so all three of them wont see him. This was a pretty good idea that he had never thought of before, but odds were it was going to work. The deal won't happen till high noon today, so D.H. will be ready for them today.

Ten minutes before noon, D.H. got out his gun and put all the bullets in it and got ready for anything that would pop out. He is looking through his window. Suddenly everybody is acting very strangely; everybody is putting bags-most likely with money inside-in the middle of the road. Somebody will take them, and D.H. knows who it is-most likely the three gangsters.

It struck high noon. D.H. is hiding in his room getting his gun ready for the shooting. Then right on time the three people come that D.H. has been waiting for. All three of them are smart guys; all three of them have covered half of their face so no one would see who they are.

All three of them got their guns out so they would be ready just in case something popped out. Less than a second later there was gunshot, and it hit right at the guns in their hands. All three of them are wondering where those gunshots were coming from, but they can't see where it was coming from. The only thing that they can do is to leave without knowing who is doing it, but they will find out sooner or later.

Right now everybody in the town is wondering who was doing that and thought to themselves that whoever the person is might be crazy and at the same time the bravest person on earth. One problem is that tonight those gangsters will come and raise havoc, but D.H. will be ready for them no matter what.

All day nobody leaves their house or other buildings because everybody is afraid to death. All of them are afraid that there's more gangsters outside waiting so they can shoot somebody, and nobody is crazy enough to go outside. Tonight everybody will be more afraid to death than before. But not D.H.-he's ready for anything that will come popping out.

One problem for D.H. is how he is going to get

out of his room in the hotel and try to outsmart those gangsters. That's one question that's been bugging the heck out of D.H. for twenty minutes. Suddenly it popped out of D.H.'s head-this is going to be crazy-but the only option he has is going through the window from the second floor tonight.

At six in the evening everybody is indoors, not crazy enough to go outside, and that's D.H.'s sign to go outside. Lucky for him that no one saw him going through the window on the second floor and jumping down. Another question for D.H. is where's a good place to hide so none of them will see him when they come in a few hours.

D.H. hid somewhere between the barbershop and the mayor's office. He got down on his knees to make sure none of them could see him and got his gun ready. Lucky for D.H. that he had extra bullets so that he would be ready for anything and for some extra help. So far this was the only safe place where he could hide so no one would see him, not even the locals.

It struck eight o'clock in the evening. D.H. was about to leave, but then something started to happen. A few people started to come in the middle of the road. There are five men, but three of them are same ones from earlier today. Seems like those guys are ready to raise havoc all over Cold Creek, and D.H. is the only one that can stop them before they can go inside and hurt somebody.

All five of them are starting to get their guns out and ready to shoot through the buildings so they can let everybody know that they are making their point-so none of them will think twice about messing with them. D.H. got out his gun, and there he goes starting to shoot them, and the gangsters don't know where the gunshots are coming from. Everybody in the town is starting to wake up and are getting down under their beds so none of them will get hurt; they aren't crazy enough to look through the window.

Two of those gangsters got shot, so the other gangsters decide to pick them up and leave, so no more of them will get hurt. Then suddenly the gunshots start to stop, and everybody is happy to death that the gunshots have stopped. D.H. has no choice but to run to his hotel room so no one will think he's the one that's doing this.

Morning came. D.H. didn't sleep all night, to make sure that none of the those gangsters came back. But when it hit eight in the morning, D.H. knew that it was safe enough to go outside. The second that D.H. went outside, he saw no living souls outside for some reason, but he understood they were afraid since last night. The only place to go to get something to eat is the local restaurant at the end of town, so D.H. goes there.

D.H. went inside the restaurant without any worries and was not surprised to see nobody inside the restaurant. He guessed that everybody was afraid to go out to eat. The only place where D.H. eats is at the back so he can see everything, and the only person that he saw was the restaurant cook.

The cook was scared half to death to go near D.H., but D.H. made sure that he was friendly, so the cook went up to him and asked him for his order. D.H. ordered steak, mashed potatoes, and milk, and he got to ask this question but acted like he didn't know anything.

"What's wrong? You act like you've seen a ghost or something," said D.H.

"All right, I'm going to sit down. Last night there was a shooting, and somebody was crazy enough to fight back at the gangsters here in this town and everybody knows right away that this person is not a local around here, cause they are more dangerous thatn any other gangsters in this country put together," said the cook.

"Maybe, just maybe, somebody is taking a stand to defend everybody in this town. Maybe it's just that," said D.H.

"Well, maybe. But whoever this person is better have good backup, because that person needs it more than ever," said the cook.

The cook leaves all worried about what's going to happen now. D.H. knows that he's dealing with something else, all right, but he isn't going to give up without a fight. Now he knows what some of those gangsters are doing around here. It's best to ask around but not ask too many questions, because he really doesn't want to cause any troubles.

THREE

FOR THE PAST few days everybody has been scared to go outside, knowing those gangster could come out anytime, raising havoc all over town after what happened with that shooting. Everybody thought to themselves that whoever pulled that crazy stunt with those gangsters must be the bravest man on earth.

Right now in the middle of the day everybody is slowly going outside and having a little fun. Everybody seems to enjoy themselves having drinks with their friends-something that they haven't enjoyed in a long time. At the same time everybody is being careful knowing that those gangsters are out there planning to do God knows what to them.

D.H. is at his hotel room planning his next idea to see who is on the right side of the law. For a person that grew up on a farm, he knew a lot about telling right from wrong. At this moment for D.H., it's best that he gets to know everybody, to see what kind of people they are and to figure out why these gangsters are different from other gangsters.

So far it's going to be very hard to see whose side is on the right side, because everybody is scared half to death to go outside. But D.H. needed to get some answers on these gangsters. The best thing to do is to watch everybody in the village one by one without anybody knowing. He has to be careful at the same time and start right now, since a few people are already outside.

Carefully, D.H. went outside without anybody knowing what he was going to do. But to play it safe, it was best to leave his gun in his room so he wouldn't scare anybody. The first person to see is the cook, since he owns a restaurant and talks to everybody. So he's the first pick of the day to see what kind of information he has. At the same time D.H. is kind of hungry, so he's going there to get something to eat.

Before D.H. could even go inside the restaurant, he saw one of the gangsters eating inside the restaurant. He doesn't want to eat at the same place with gangster. The only thing to do is to walk away and pretend that he doesn't know anything. There's go to be a good reason why that gangster is so close to the town. Maybe he's spying to find out who shot them that night. D.H. has to be careful.

D.H. went back to his room, got his gun out, and

put it where all cowboys do-near his waist-just in case. Luckily for D.H., he stayed relaxed so no one would know what he was doing. Besides, this is the Old West, he thought to himself, and he needs his gun. Now he goes back to the restaurant to see if he can get some answers before all havoc breaks loose.

Everything seems like normal. That gangster is just eating his meal, with not a care in the world. This very strange, but D.H. makes sure that the gangster won't know that he's following his track. Also, the last thing that he wants is somebody getting hurt, because D.H. has a good soul inside of him and this is what God sent him to do-to help people.

D.H. ordered his meal and calmly finished it without any trouble. The gangsters is seated all the way in the front, and D.H. is seated all the way in back so he can keep a close eye on him. So far, the gangster is minding his own business, but at the same time looking for some answers about the shooting a few nights ago. The gangster wants revenge on the person who tried to kill them.

It seems like the gangster is going nowhere, so the best thing to do is to leave Cold Creek for now but come back later to get some answers about the shooting. D.H., on the other hand, decided not to follow him, because odds are he's going to look behind him and get his head blown off.

It looks like nobody knows who that person is, by the way everybody is acting. When the gangster stepped out of the restaurant, not even the cook knew who it was, so the cook is out because he didn't know that gangster. D.H. doesn't know how lucky he is that the gangster doesn't know what he looks like, but D.H. has to be extra careful next time so no one will know what he's doing.

Every day for the past week, D.H. interviewed everybody in the whole city. It seems like everybody felt relaxed and not bugged at all; nobody suspected what D.H. was doing . Right away, everybody is marked clean. Nobody is helping the gangsters out. So right now it's between the gangsters and D.H.-nobody else.

One problem still remained. Why are these gangsters raising havoc here is this town, and what makes these gangsters different from other gangsters?. D.H. is going to get some more answers, but at the same time he's going to be careful about what he's going to do. The last thing that he wants is for somebody to suspect what he's going to do.

In the nighttime D.H. hasn't gone to bed yet. He's trying to put the pieces together here in Cold Creek. Suddenly, D.H. heard something outside. It sounded like something dropped, and it came from downstairs. He decided to investigate before anything got stolen.

D.H. got out through the window and jumped from the second floor. Luckily for him, the person who was making all that noise didn't see him. Whoever that person was started coming near him. The only place that he could hide was the side of the building. That person started to come closer and closer. D.H. jumped the guy and managed to hold him down.

"All right, I'll talk, whoever you are, but please don't hurt me," said the stranger.

"Who are you? What's the meaning of all this racket you are making down here?" said D.H.

"My name is Butch Sundown, and I've got some information about your case, D.H.," said Butch.

"How did you know my name and what I'm doing?" said D.H.

"Never mind that. It doesn't matter how I know. Don't worry. I'm the only one that knows. I won't tell a soul," said Butch.

"All right, and thank you for helping me out. Now please tell me," said D.H.

"Tonight is the only night that I'm going to help you, and you will never see me again. The reason why those gangsters are after this town is because there isn't much law around here," said Butch.

"It could explain why everybody is afraid to speak out, but I got to ask one question....Why isn't there any sheriff around here to uphold the law?" said D.H.

"Like you said, everybody is afraid. But the government doesn't have much law around here to help the good people of Cold Creek," said Butch.

"Yeah, I see. Thank you for telling me. You may go now, and don't worry I'll pretend that I never saw you before," said D.H.

"Thank you. I won't forget about this," said Butch.

Butch calmly but carefully left Cold Creek, and nobody ever heard from him again, not even D.H. D.H. finally had some answers about what was going on and why everybody was so afraid. There's got to be some law here in Cold Creek, D.H. thought to himself.

Right now, D.H. is known in and around Cold Creek and he knows everybody. But he can't take the chance of everybody knowing what he's going to do with those gangsters. Luckily, there were no Indians around in this part of the land for some reason.

The best thing to do now is to find out where those gangsters are hiding out. D.H. knows how to take them on one by one, but Cold Creek is a big area, and so far, D.H. doesn't know where to start to find them. D.H. will start tomorrow night when everybody is asleep and no one will know, but right now he needs some rest. Tomorrow night D.H. will be on a lookout.

The next night came. D.H. had stayed in his room the whole day, minding his own business but spending a lot of time thinking about where to get started. He decided that the best place to start was North Cold Creek, because D.H. remembered that those gangsters he shot that night went north, so maybe that's where they were. He hoped that there weren't any surprises tonight like what he did to those gangsters that night.

Luckily for D.H., everybody is sound asleep so no one will give him a hard time about tonight or what he is going to do. D.H. looked everywhere. On the first places north, west, east, and south, the only thing that the could find was mountains. So far, D.H. didn't find anything, not even campfire, to show where those gangsters went. So the best thing to do is to go back to town so no one will think that he left.

FOUR

SINCE D.H. DIDN'T find anything last night, he wondered where those gangsters came from. Sooner or later he's going to find out that somebody watched and followed him last night. Luckily for D.H., the person didn't see what he looks like, so he's safe for now.

It's high noon in the Northeast Country five miles from Cold Creek. There's a meeting here with all of the gangsters. The leader of the gang is Thomas "The Killer," one of the most dangerous as Jesse James.

Right now, Thomas "The Killer" is pretty angry about what happened a week ago-about the shooting and that his men didn't do the job. So far, nobody has said a word, but somehow he always knows these kinds of things. So it's best that he do most of the talking, since none of them is crazy enough to outsmart him.

"I heard what happened last week. Right now, I'm pretty angry-enough to kill each and every one of you guys. Now start explaining. Who was this person that's crazy enough to take use on?" said Thomas.

"We don't know. It's got to be somebody new, `cause nobody in that town is crazy enough to take use on, and all three of us know that it isn't Indians," said Outlaw 1.

"Yeah, I know that it isn't the Indians, `cause there isn't any Indians around here in Cold Creek. Guys, don't tell me something that I do know; tell me something I don't know. But I know for a fact that it's somebody new, all right," said Thomas.

"That's all we know, Thomas, `cause everybody in town already knows us and isn't crazy enough to take us on," said Outlaw 2.

"You're not getting any disagreement on that subject. All right, here's the thing. We are going to get some new people to join us. They will go down there to do some investigating, and no one will know our plan," said Thomas.

"That's a good idea, but one question. Who do we know that's willing to join us? Everybody in the whole town knows us pretty well," said Outlaw 3.

"Good question. I'm way ahead of you on that. I already hired somebody to do the job. His name is Frank Lopez," said Thomas.

All three of the gangsters looked behind them and saw Frank Lopez; all three of them had to admit he looked very dangerous. Frank knew right away that he could easily take all three of them on.

"You know what to do?" said Thomas.

"Yes," said Frank.

Frank got onto his horse and rode all the way to Cold Creek. Not wasting any time, Frank started to look around and decided to go to the post office to check the mail for anybody that was getting outside mail.

He was inside the post office when suddenly D.H came inside. He didn't notice Frank and calmly got his mail. But then Frank notices the letter and that it came from Fort Worth, Texas. Frank thought to himself, *Why would somebody get a letter all the way from Forth Worth, Texas?* He decides to follow this person.

Calmly following D.H., Frank pretends that he's minding his own business and follows D.H. without any trouble. D.H. went inside the restaurant and so did Frank. They sat across from each other. Without any trouble Frank read the letter, and D.H. had no idea that he was sitting across from a gangster.

It turns out that the letter is nothing. He decides the best thing to do is to order something to eat so that the person won't know what he's doing. Frank wants is any surprises. Luckily for Frank, there aren't any wanted posters with his face on them. He doesn't want to blow his cover.

Frank checked everywhere in Cold Creek, and nobody knew who the son of a gun was who did that shooting last week. He decided to do a shooting that evening so everybody would know not to mess with them ever again-not even the mysterious person, whoever he is.

Nighttime was coming near, and that was usually a sign for everybody to go inside. Little did they know that there would be hell happening tonight. Even D.H. doesn't know; it's going to be a very big surprise for him also.

At eight in the evening all four of the gangsters got onto their horses and rode as fast as they could all the way to Cold Creek. They made it to the middle of the town, pulled their guns out, and started to shoot right through the buildings to get everybody to wake up. In less than a second everybody woke up and knew that it was those gangsters.

Ten minutes passed, and those gangsters finished shooting and left. Everybody made sure to not to follow them again. Even D.H. woke up from all the gunshots. He wasn't going to give up that easily, but it was a miracle that no one got hurt from all this. If there was only a way that D.H. could get some help, even from the Indians would be great.

At three in the morning D.H. went back to be, but the rest of the town were afraid to go back to sleep. But the children had no trouble going back to bed. D.H. got up at ten in the morning and noticed a note on top of the desk saying, *"You are on the right track. Me and my people are here you. Meet us a sundown two miles Northeast of Cold Creek. Signed, A Friend."*

Judging from the writing, it came from an Indian. But that was impossible, as there weren't any Indians here in this part of the land-or were there? So tonight D.H. is going to visit a new friend. D.H. is hoping that this person is all right, because the lost thing he needs is a gunshot to the head. The best thing to do is not to tell anybody about tonight and to go alone without anybody knowing.

The sun went down, and soon everybody in the town was sound asleep. D.H. left the town and went two miles Northeast without any trouble. Nobody even followed him. He made it to the area that the person had mentioned, when suddenly D.H. heard something.

"Whoever you are, come on out. I heard you," said D.H.

The person came out. It was an Indian. D.H. put his gun down so he didn't want to take any chances. The Indian came closer and closer, and D.H. made himself relax to show the Indian that he didn't want to hurt him. Suddenly the Indian stopped fifteen inches away.

"Are you the one who sent the note to my room in Cold Creek?" said D.H.

"Yes. I'm Desert Fox. The reason why I send for you that note that is the gangster that you are looking for killed my family. His name is Thomas "The Killer." Me and my people are willing to help you. Also, I know that Thomas has help also, scaring the people of Cold Creek," said Desert Fox.

"I'm willing to accept you and your people's help," said D.H.

"Thank you so much. You have earned the trust and respect of my people," said Desert Fox.

"Oh, thank you. But I've got to ask you one question. Why don't any other Indians live around here? Everybody in town told me there aren't any around" said D.H.

"Same here. I also don't know where they are, but that's why we will work together," said Desert Fox.

"All right, keep me up to date on everything , and I'll keep you up to date about everybody in the town," said D.H.

"I understand, and thank you for helping me and my people. I must go now. My people need me. Thank you for meeting me here," said Desert Fox.

"You're welcome, Desert Fox. I'll see you later," said D.H.

Desert Fox turned around and mysteriously disappeared into thin air. D.H. had never seen anything like that before. Somehow D.H. knew he would treasure his friendship with his new friend. It's just a feeling he has inside his soul. It's best that he goes back right away so no one will know that he was out talking with somebody to frighten off those evil gangsters.

FIVE

It's been very quiet in Cold Creek. It seems like everybody is afraid to leave their houses, even to go see their friends, knowing that those gangsters are out there planning something to get even. D.H., in his room at the hotel, can't help wondering what else is going to happen. So far, D.H. feels like he is responsible for what happens here in Cold Creek; it's a miracle that nobody has gotten hurt so far.

After twenty minutes of wondering, D.H. finally got it. Those gangsters are not attacking; they are waiting for him to leave. That shooting was just a warning. No warning is going to scare D.H. out of town. It isn't going work. D.H. has been sent here for a reason, and he's going to help to everybody in town, whether those gangsters like it or not.

Meanwhile, up at the northeast area of Cold Creek, those gangsters are having another meeting; but this meeting is a little different. The difference is that at the river there is an Indian hiding behind the rocks, and he can overhear everything that the gangsters are saying. The Indian is a member of the Desert Fox group, and he and D.H. are about the get a heads-up on what is going to happen next.

"That was some shooting a few nights ago, but we have to find out who is trying to fight us off," said Thomas.

"Tell me about it; when I went through Cold Creek, everybody was scared half to death. That's a good sign," said Frank.

"It is, but we can't get our hopes up yet. Whoever this person is, most likely he's still there planning something," said Thomas.

"What are we going to do next?" said Gangster 1.

"Good question. We are going to plan another surprise attack again tomorrow night at midnight," said Thomas.

"It's a good idea," said Gangster 2.

The rest of them agreed on what Gangster 2 said. Tomorrow night they would make another surprise attack on Cold Creek. Little did those gangsters know that an Indian overheard everything they said. Right away he was very careful, but as fast as he could he rode all the way to tell what he heard to Desert Fox.

None of those gangsters saw him leave; he knew that if they did see him, those gangsters would shoot and kill him. As fast as he could, he made it to the Indian area where all of his friends and family were. Right away, he went up to Desert Fox and told him what he had heard. Desert Fox was glad that those gangsters didn't hurt him and had given him the information.

The never evening, D.H. and Desert Fox's men were hiding all over Cold Creek. Before the shooting D.H. prayed for the people of Cold Creek and his new Indian friends to be safe. The last thing that he wanted was for somebody to get hurt.

At eleven o'clock at night all four of the gangsters are in the middle of the road. They pull their guns out and are about to shoot the buildings. Less than a second after they started, the gangsters got a big surprise. Somebody started to shoot at them from different directions. They can't see who's doing it, because it's very dark.

"What are we going to do, Thomas?" We don't know who the shooter is," said Gangster 1.

"Same here. Whoever this person is has help from the locals. Best thing to do is to leave before we get ourselves killed. Let's go," said Thomas.

All of them left the area before one of them could get killed, but at the same time they were wondering who the shooters were. When everybody saw them leaving, all of the locals started cheering. D.H. thanked the Indians for all their help. All of them got a big laugh from how the gangsters had reacted.

Morning came. To play it safe, D.H. stayed indoors. Suddenly D.H. heard something outside; an arrow was stuck right near the window with a note on it. He knows right away that it's a message from Desert Fox.

The note said, *"Meet me tonight at the same spot as last time. Come alone and be careful."*

D.H. remembered the last time he met Desert Fox. D.H. wondered what he wanted; maybe it wasn't that serious, or maybe it was. The question is, how he's going to leave without anybody noticing that he's leaving. The best thing to do is to wait until tonight and see what would happen. Maybe he would get lucky and leave without any trouble.

The day passed an evening came. D.H. left the building, got onto his horse, and took off for the same place as before. Twenty minutes passed, and D.H. made it to the same place at the same time without any trouble. A few more minutes passed, and D.H. saw Desert Fox coming toward him alone.

"How are you doing, my friend ?" said Desert Fox.

"I'm doing well. Thank you for asking. What about you, and what do you need me for?" said D.H.

"I'm doing well. Thank you for asking. The reason I need to talk to you is to thank you for helping me and my people, and I want to make sure that you are all right," said Desert Fox.

"You're welcome, my friend, and I'm doing well. Thank you for caring, but I'm sure that you need me for something else, so please tell me," said D.H.

"Yes, there is something else I need to ask you . I need a favor from you," said Desert Fox.

"Well, tell me. That's why I'm here, my friend," said D.H.

"When we get Thomas "The Killer," I'm the one that wants to kill him. He took something away from me, and I want him personally. Do you understand?" said Desert Fox.

"I understand. You may kill him; he's all yours," said D.H.

"Thank you. I won't forget about this. You truly are a good friend. I must go now," said Desert Fox.

"Well, I'm glad that we had this talk. I'll see you later," said D.H.

Both of them left the area without any trouble. D.H. had no trouble getting inside his hotel room. He was glad that he had the talk with Desert Fox. D.H. understood Desert Fox's feelings on this. They both were working on defending the town during these hard times. He hoped that one day Desert Fox would invite him to his place.

SIX

TWO DAYS AGO was something, all right with D.H. and Desert Fox fighting off those gangsters and catching them by surprise. Both of them go a big laugh out of this, but little did D.H. know that he would have a little problem soon. Morning came and D.H. was pretty hungry, so he went to the restaurant to get something to eat.

The cook was afraid but glad to be alive. But one thing that D.H. doesn't understand is how the cook managed to continue running the restaurant, since there aren't that many people coming inside. That went for everybody else in town. How did everything run without anybody going in?

"What would you like to have today?" said the cook.

"I would like to have pancakes, eggs, and a cup of coffee, please," said D.H.

D.H. can't blame the cook for being so scared, since the shooting was just a few days ago. D.H. has to stay relaxed and pretend to act like everybody else. D.H. doesn't like pretending to act like something he's not. The cook delivered D.H's meal, and he asked the cook to join him. D.H. needs to talk, and it seems like the cook is willing to.

"Just relax. I'm not going to hurt you. Besides, I came here a couple of times, so please relax," said D.H.

"All right, I do need a break. I'll tell you one thing-whoever started that shooting a few nights ago must be the bravest men on earth," said the cook.

"Is that what everybody in town think?" said D.H.

"Oh, yeah. Everybody is saying that," said the cook.

"That's good to hear. At least somebody is looking out for the little guys, so we've got nothing to worry about," said D.H.

"I don't know about that. I feel like everybody's life is in danger, knowing that those gangsters will come back, but this time angrier and finish us off," said the cook.

"They're not going to kill us. Whoever this person is, he is trying to help us. You and everybody else have got to understand that. Who would come all this way to help us out?" said D.H.

"Yeah, that's the truth all right. But there's a lot of questions about this," said the cook.

"What question?" said D.H.

"You know what question," said the cook.

"No, I don't. Please tell me," said D.H.

"There's a lot of different questions. All kinds. You name it, they're saying it, and I'm having a hard time keeping track of it," said the cook.

"I don't know what to say about this, but thank you for the meal," said D.H.

D.H. left the restaurant without any worries, but he wondered what the cook meant about the questions all over town. Since everybody in town was starting to ask questions, D.H. needed to get some answers right away before things got out of hand. The last thing that D.H. wants is to be backed into a corner.

Slowly, everybody is starting to come out of their houses. D.H. had no trouble fitting in around town. The first thing that D.H. thought to himself was that the cook sure wasn't joking around about everybody starting to ask questions about the shooting a few nights ago. D.H. tried to answers as many questions as he could while at the same time trying to stay relaxed and not let everybody know what he's doing.

Suddenly, the may started to come up to D.H. D.H. started to notice the mayor coming up to him, but D.H. hoped that Mayor Jacobson didn't know it was him and a couple of Indians who had done the shooting a few nights ago.

"Hi, D.H. How are you doing this lovely morning?" said Mayor Jacobson.

"I'm doing well. Thank you for asking. What about you?" said D.H.

"Same here. Feeling great. That was some shooting a few nights ago," said Mayor Jacobson.

"Yeah, that was something all right," said D.H.

"A few nights ago I think I saw some of the people who were shooting.....or maybe I didn't, since it was nighttime and you could hardly see what they looked like," said D.H.

"I guess you're right, D.H., but the bottom line is nobody got hurt. I'm hoping that one day Cold Creek will be a peaceful town again before those gangsters came here," said Mayor Jacobson.

"Same here, Mayor Jacobson," said D.H.

That was a close one. For second there, the mayor almost found out what really happened a few nights ago and who was doing the shooting. Right now, everybody is still asking questions about the shootings. D.H. is running out of answers, but he answers them the best way he can. After this long day finally came to an end, D.H. was hoping that there was no more surprises tonight, because he wanted to go to bed.

SEVEN

A FEW DAYS PASSED without any trouble. D.H. might have made his point to those gangsters, but he wasn't getting his hopes up at all. He knew that gangsters don't give up easily. They always have a way to fight back when somebody messes with one of them, or all of them. But D.H. is ready for anything, and so is his friend Desert Fox.

Luckily for him and the Indians, nobody in town saw what they look like at the shooting a week ago, when D.H. and Desert Fox and some of his friends outsmarted those gangsters that night. Also, everybody was asking a lot of questions about the shooting that night, and D.H. was running out of answers to give to everybody in town. Right now, D.H. is wondering what those gangsters are doing right about now, so he can be ready for anything that they will bring to raise havoc here in Cold Creek.

It seems like everybody is getting over their fear about leaving their homes. They are sure that somebody is trying to help them through these hard times when the gangsters rule all over Cold Creek. Even the mayor feels much better also about upholding the law and taking care of his hometown by making a few laws that the put on the wall near the restaurant. D.H. went up to see it, just like everybody else was. The law said:

1. Report any illegal guns to the mayor.
2. Report any gangsters in Cold Creek.
3. No shoplifting or stealing.

Those are some of the rules that D.H. is reading. So far, everybody in town is blocking his view, but he doesn't care at long as he and the Indians are making a differences here in Cold Creek. The best thing to do is to leave. Everybody else wants to look at all the new laws that have been brought to their town. Somebody is making a difference, and they don't care who the person is.

D.H. thought to himself that he wouldn't be surprised to see a wanted poster of the gangsters, so everybody in town will be ready to fight back, or maybe D.H. and the Indians will. Right now up at the northeast area away from Cold Creek, the gangsters are having some serious talk about what's going on in Cold Creek.

"I just can't believe that they are making some

changes in Cold Creek. I just can't believe it. This is making me more and more angry. If I only knew the guy who is making the difference down there, I would personally shoot him to death. If only I could find him…." said Thomas.

"What are we going to do? If they get those new laws down there, odds are they are going to put wanted posters with our faces on them and we will really be in hot water," said Gangster 1.

"I know, I know, but I'm thinking of something to outsmart those people down at Cold Creek. Before this guy came along, we owned that town," said Thomas.

"We could do another shooting, but whoever that person is will be ready for us, so that's out of the question," said Gangster 2.

"And you're lucky-you're the very first person that has ever asked me," said D.H.

"My name has a meaning also. I'm fast as a fox and I grew up in the desert. That's how I got my name Desert Fox," said Desert Fox.

"That's wonderful. I'll bet you know a lot of stuff from the past and you lead your people," said D.H.

"It's true. I have a lot of wisdom for my age. That's why I'm the leader of my people. And I know for sure that you are young. Why did somebody so young come here?" said Desert Fox.

"It's a long story, but I'll make it short. I wanted to start my adventure-something new in life. Don't get me wrong. I miss my home in Forth Worth, Texas, but everybody picks their own path. Do you understand why, Desert Fox?" said D.H.

"Yes, I do. Everybody needs to pick their own path in life-even me and the rest of the Indians here in this country," said Desert Fox.

Both of them smiled and laughed pretty hard, and they stayed up all night talking. Both of them are having a good time hanging out and becoming good friends and getting to know each other. The sun is about to come up, so both of them decide to leave. But they didn't leave without saying good-bye and shaking hands.

Luckily for both of them, nobody saw them or watched them-not even Thomas and his gang. D.H. had to admit one thing: he hadn't had that much fun talking to somebody in a long time, and it kind of felt good.

D.H. got back to town, and everybody seemed to be awake and fresh. But one person was wondering why D.H. came back into town. There had to be a good reason, so he decided to go up and ask him, because the mayor is a caring person who cares about others he cares about himself. D.H. notices that the mayor is starting to come up to him, and he's hoping and praying inside that he won't ask him why he is coming into town. If he does, D.H. has no choices but to lie.

"Good morning, Mayor. How can I help you out today?" said D.H.

"I was wondering why you were coming into town. Were you up all night?" said Mayor Jacobson.

"I couldn't sleep, so I decided to go on a horse ride. I'm sorry if I scared you in any way," said D.H.

"That could explain why you came into town. I'm glad that you are all right and that nothing serious happened to you from those gangsters out there, planning who knows what to us. The next time if you are going out for a ride, please tell me, would you-so just in case you are missing or hurt, I'll know where to be to help you," said Mayor Jacobson.

"Don't worry. I'll remember. Thank you for caring, Mayor," said D.H.

The mayor walked away, and D.H. thought to himself, That was a close one. The last thing that he wants is somebody causing trouble. D.H. feels bad. He's not used to lying, and he hopes that he will never lie again. Right now, he's going to his hotel room to get some rest, since he didn't sleep all night. He thought to himself that he earned it without any worries.

EIGHT

LAST NIGHT WAS something that D.H. will never forget, spending time with his new friend Desert Fox. It's lucky for D.H. that no one will ever find out about last night. Not even the mayor will ever know, and usually the mayor is the first to know about everything. D.H. is very lucky, and he wondered to himself how lucky one person could get. But he isn't going to push his luck that much, because you can't always depend on luck.

Meanwhile back in the Indian area where Desert Fox is hanging out and staying, he is sitting near the campfire wondering how he's going to get Thomas "The Killer." Desert Fox is still so angry, and more than anything Desert Fox wants revenge for what he has done to him and his people.

One problem for Desert Fox is that he doesn't know

where the killer is hiding out, but he wants to rest until he finds him and he'll personally take care of him. Desert Fox and D.H. have a strong agreement that Desert Fox will personally take care of him when they find him. One problem is that the both of them don't know where he and those gangsters are hiding, but they're hoping that soon they will find him.

So far, none of the Indians knows what is bugging Desert Fox, and so far Desert Fox doesn't want anybody to know. This is to personal for him, so no one will ever be crazy enough to ask him. The only person that knows Desert Fox's secret is D.H., and he trusted him with his life.

Right now at Cold Creek, D.H. is thinking something similar about where Thomas "The Killer" is hiding out. D.H. is willing to help everybody in Cold Creek thinking about it over and over. Sooner or later, he and Desert Fox will find him, and D.H. promised Desert Fox that he'll take care of him personally.

Late that night, Desert Fox made it to the cemetery where his wife was buried. She passed away five years ago, but he promised her that he would avenge her for what Thomas "The Killer" did all those years ago. Then suddenly Desert Fox heard something like somebody was coming near to him. It was lucky that he had his gun with him.

A second later, Desert Fox turned around and saw his old enemy, Thomas "The Killer," smiling at him. But Desert Fox is ready for anything, even if his gangs are around him. Thomas "The Killer" is staying a good distant away from Desert Fox and both have there guns out ready for anything.

"It's been a long time, old friend," said Thomas.

"We're not old friends. You murder my wife and children every single day of my life. I think about killing you for what you have done," said Desert Fox.

"I'll do it all over again if I wanted to, so don't do anything stupid like finding me, `cause I'm always one step ahead of you," said Thomas.

"We will see about that. This time I've got help, and I'm going to outsmart you like you did to em all those years ago," said Desert Fox.

"Oh, so you've got some help. That could explain that shooting a few weeks ago-you have help. If it's a war you want, a war you will get. Good-bye," said Thomas.

Desert Fox didn't say a word. He's going to be ready for anything that pops out. Thomas "The Killer" disappeared into the dark. Desert Fox never thought that he would have a face-to-face talk with his enemy. It's best for him that he will not say a word about this to anyone, because the last thing he wants is somebody worrying about him.

After a whole hour, Desert Fox decided to leave the cemetery. So far this has got to be the strangest and most dangerous experience that he ever had in his whole life, but he's glad he came out of it alive. He came right back to the same spot as before without saying a word about where he went. Desert Fox doesn't want anybody to worry about him to much.

Meanwhile back at town, the mayor notices D.H.

coming near the restaurant, so the mayor decides to join him. So far, he's still wondering what D.H. was doing the other night. D.H. notices that the mayor is following him, so the best thing to is to stay relaxed. He's got nothing to lose. Maybe the mayor wants to join him for breakfast or something.

"Hi, Mayor Jacobson. How are you doing this lovely morning? Care to join me for breakfast?" said Mayor Jacobson.

"Yeah, I'll join you. It would be pretty nice to have the company for a change," said Mayor Jacobson.

"All right, It's on me today, Mayor," said D.H.

"Oh, thank you," said Mayor Jacobson.

Both of them enjoyed their breakfast, but for sure D.H. knew that he was going to ask about a few nights ago. But D.H. remained relaxed, pretending that he didn't know anything. The mayor knows everything that goes around here in Cold Creek, so it's best to keep things to himself about that night.

Both of them finished their meals, and the good mayor didn't say a word about that night. It's best to mind his won business. But somehow the mayor will find out that he's the one that's been helping everybody by fighting off those gangsters. The only thing that he can do is to stay out of it until D.H. asks for some help. But the mayor knows that he is keeping things under control, but he's hoping that on one will get hurt.

This is the Old Wild West. People don't run away from their problems. They fight their problems out in the open. That's what the mayor was thinking. Right now, the mayor is thanking God for delivering somebody like D.H. So far, the mayor is going to thank his lucky stars if he's right about D.H.

Nighttime came. D.H. spent all day in his room worried half to death knowing that the mayor might be on to him. Right now, D.H. is walking back and forth all worried to death trying to think things through. The last thing that he wants is to go to jail, or much worse, get hanged. Maybe-just maybe-he should got to the mayor and have a talk with him about it. But no, D.H. thought to himself. He could get into a lot of trouble for this so it was best to keep it to himself and Desert Fox.

From now on, D.H. has to be careful so no one will find out what's going to happen. The last thing that he wants is somebody getting hurt or much worse. So far, D.H. is hoping that Desert Fox doesn't have this much trouble with his people. He'll hate himself if anything bad happens to him.

NINE

RIGHT NOW, IT'S pretty shaky with what's going on with D.H. and Desert Fox. Both of them are in hot water, but they have to keep each other informed on what's happening with the enemies and with the mayor of Cold Creek. D.H. knows for sure that Desert Fox will contact him later on today about whether it's safe or not to meet tonight. So far, they need to work something out, to put their heads together to get out of this jam.

All day, D.H. remained normal, pretending nothing is bugging him at all. But he's hoping that he gets a note to meet Desert Fox tonight at the same time and same place. Right behind him is good old Mayor Jacobson. He's a nice guy all right, but he wants to make sure that he's wrong-that D.H. isn't trying to take on the gangsters all by himself. Somehow, D.H. has to outsmart him, but

D.H. will find out tonight if he's going to meet Desert Fox. He's hoping that the mayor will find out tonight if he's going to meet Desert Fox. He's hoping that the mayor will be sound asleep and wont know what he's going to do.

D.H, acting very relaxed, pretending not to have a care in the world, and knowing that the mayor is right behind him. After a long day passed, D.H. decided to go to his hotel room. Luckily for him, he's a pretty good jumper, jumping down from the second floor to his feet without any trouble.

He calmly went inside the hotel without any worries, and right where D.H. was waiting, there was a note on top of the desk near his bed. The note said, *"Meet me at the same place at the same time. Come alone. I have been though enough already, and I don't want any surprises. From Desert Fox."*

It looks important, and he sounds like he's been through enough already these past few days, just what he has been through with the mayor these past few days. The question is how to escape, knowing that the mayor is out there watching him like a hawk. Then suddenly D.H. remembered he could go though the back without any trouble. So far the mayor hasn't checked the back. Nobody does here in this town of Cold Creek.

Tonight for sure he's sneaking out without any trouble. D.H. has never outsmarted a mayor before, but there is a first time for everything in life. At eight in the evening everybody locked their doors and windows so nobody could break into their home, even those gangsters-and that goes double for the mayor. D.H. went behind the hotel building and snuck out without anybody knowing, go onto his horse, and took off without any trouble.

Right on time there is Desert Fox, but he looks pretty angry, so this is going to be one of those talks that those two won't forget. D.H. got down from his horse and right away got down to the business of what those two are going to talk about.

"What's the matter, Desert Fox? It looks like you saw a ghost or something," said D.H.

"I had a close encounter with Thomas a few night ago, and believe me, it isn't something you would like," said Desert Fox.

"Believe me, I can understand how you feel about talking to that monster, but I don't understand one thing. Why didn't you shoot him when you had the chance?" said D.H.

"That's a good question, and I don't know. But I should of shot him when I had the chance," said Desert Fox.

"Don't worry about it. If it's hard for you to talk about, you don't have to say anything. I'm an understanding person. But I'm going to some problems down at Cold Creek," said D.H.

"What kind of problems?" said Desert Fox.

"It's that mayor that's making me crazy. I have to sneak out so he won't follow me. I got to tell you the truth, I can't deal with this anymore. But I'm not complaining at all," said D.H.

"I can understand why that would make you go crazy. But I'm glad that you are not complaining, `cause only a nutcase complains all the time," said Desert Fox.

"Tell me about it. I'm not used to complaining all the time, but I need your help, Desert Fox. What should I do?" said D.H.

"Stay low and act normal. At the same time, me and my people will take care of the town on our own. All right?" said Desert Fox.

"All right, I'll do that. Thank you. But I got to ask you a quick question. What about you?" said D.H.

"don't you worry about me. I'll be alright…But thank you for caring, D.H.," said Desert Fox.

You're welcome, Desert Fox." said D.H.

Meanwhile where the gangster are hiding, they are having their own private meeting at this very moment. Thomas is all smiles knowing that he got to Desert Fox. This is going be a meeting that Thomas will be happy with. However they are currently getting down to business. There is something he needs to talk about.

"All right, guys, we need to get down to business on this. We have to do something about Cold Creek. I know that the town is getting help from Indians here in these parts." said Thomas.

"Indians?! That's impossible!!" There aren't any Indians here in this part of the country," said Frank.

"Well there are. Most likely they are ready for us. I don't know how," said Thomas.

"Why us?" said Gangster 1.

"Let's just say that there is some unfinished business between me and one of them," said Thomas.

"That could explain the shooting a week ago. I know that there was more than one person doing the shooting," said Gangster 2.

"Pretty much, but most likely those Indians have help from inside town, but sooner or later we'll find out. We're going to make a little visit, and it's going to be one that those people will never forget," said Gangster 3.

All day the next day, D.H. is acting very relaxed, pretending that he doesn't know anything about the Indians or about the shooting a week ago. Little does nobody know that tonight there will be a shooting, but the Indians will help them out, and the mayor will back off from D.H.

The day passed and nighttime came. The mayor went outside and decided to go to D.H.'s hotel room to see that he doesn't do anything crazy, and to see for himself that he's wrong- Which he's hoping. The mayor knocks on the door. D.H. is not surprised to see the mayor at his front door. Most likey D.H. is thinking that he's checking up with him.

"Mayor Jacobson, what a surpise. Come on in," said D.H.

"Well thank you, I thought I should stop by to pay you a visit. I'm hoping that this isn't a bad time," said Mayor Jacobson.

"Not at all. I'm glad that you came. It's nice to have some visitors come in. I haven't had one - well not just yet. You are my first one. What have you been up to?" said D.H.

"Oh, nothing much. I'm just happy that somebody is trying to frighten those gangsters out of town. It's crazy but good that somebody is helping the town a bit," said the mayor.

"Tell me about it. Since I first moved here from Fort Worth, this town has been downhill. But whoever this person is, is helping everybody out pretty good. I wish I could shake the person's hand on this," said D.H.

"Same here. It makes my job a lot easier. I have been trying to get a sheriff to frighten off those gangsters, but I'm glad that we've got some extra help to fight off those gangsters," said Mayor Jacobson.

Right before D.H. could say anything, both of them heard gunshots outside. The only thing that D.H. can do is to turn off the lights of the candles so no one knows who is in the room. The second thing is to watch outside to see what's going on and pray that no one will shoot them to death or even come inside.

Mayor Jacobson is very impresses that somebody is fighting off those gangsters, and glad that he is wrong about D.H. fighting off those gangsters. One problem that's bugging the mayor is who is shooting at the gangsters. It's so dark that the mayor can't see who it is. But whoever it is, the mayor is thinking, has got to be the greatest group of people on Earth.

The gangsters, on the other hand, are having a hard time seeing who is shooting at them. They're keeping them busy and slowly going up to them to see who is doing this. One of the gangsters is coming near one of the Indians near the alley next to the bar, but there's one problem: the Indian knows he's coming near him.

The best thing to do is stop shooting and start running into the alley next to the bar, into the darkness without any trace. The gangster started to run after him. When he made it to the end of the alley, the gangster looked both ways to see where he went, and suddenly the Indian hit him right in the face. The gangster was right on the ground and didn't move a muscle. The Indian ran away so no one would see him.

Those gangsters decided to give up and run away. They are going to leave their other member and deal with him later. None of them wants to get killed from all the gun shooting by surprise. So far, nobody got any sleep that night, but they're glad that there isn't any more shooting and glad that nobody got hurt and that the mayor safely made it to his home.

Morning came. Everybody calmly made it outside. All of them looked everywhere, but at the same time were careful. They don't want any surprises. D.H. and the mayor went inside the alley where the bar was and weren't surprised to see one of the gangsters on the ground. They guess that somebody hit him, but D.H. knows it was one of the Indians giving a sign of their help.

The best thing to do is to take this gangster to jail and ask him a lot of questions about where those other gangsters are. It's best for D.H. to stay away from him so he wont tell the other gangsters who he is, so they won't hunt him down and kill him. D.H. is very happy about what the Indians did, and right before D.H. could leave got to his hotel room, the mayor said he was sorry about what he did. D.H. said that it was all right.

In D.H.'s hotel room he's hoping that his good friend Desert Fox is all right and that his friends are all right. He's hoping that nothing bad happened to them, but at the same time glad that one of those gangsters is behind bars. Maybe Thomas "The Killer" knows that they mean business.

The gangsters woke up but wasn't surprised that he was in a jail cell. He knows that the other gangsters will help him out. The best thing that he's going to do is to keep quiet and not tell a soul where his hideout is. But most likely they moved somewhere else so nobody in the town will find out. He's thinking about what to do right now.

TEN

AFTER A FEW days passed, they decide to hire a sheriff in town, but they don't know how after they captured a dangerous fugitive, who's on their hands inside the county jail. The mayor is the only one that isn't afraid to talk to the fugitive, and that fugitive's name is Robert Donner. Robert Donner is wanted for murder, and he's been on the run for more than five years. The people in town are glad that they got one of those gangsters off the streets so he won't hurt anybody else.

There still is one problem on their hands, for everybody in Cold Creek knows by now that those gangsters are still out there planning something to get even with whoever did this to him. But nobody knows who is doing this. Nobody is afraid anymore to go outside. Everybody has the confidence to go outside and enjoy their day.

One problem that's still bugging everybody in Cold Creek is who is crazy enough to talk to the fugitive. Everybody in Cold Creek knows that it can't be the mayor, because they mayor has to take care of the town like very other mayor in this country. D.H. really wishes he could talk to the fugitive, because he isn't afraid. But he can't interfere until the job is really done, by taking care of all those gangsters.

The mayor is in his office walking back and forth, wondering who is crazy enough to talk to the fugitive without getting scared half to death. Mayor Jacobson needs a sheriff badly, but who is going to be the lucky one to take on this kind of responsibility? Luckily for the mayor, he didn't get angry at people outside of his office yelling at him about this.

The best thing to do is to keep this fugitive behind bars until they find somebody crazy enough to do this without get scared half to death. Boy, the mayor wishes that he has a sheriff at his hand for something like this. D.H. already knows what's going on with everybody, and he could possibly understand how everybody feels about this.

Mayor Jacobson is going to do something that no mayor has ever done before: he's going to interview the fugitive tonight. Right now, the mayor is going to write a letter to the governor saying that they've got a fugitive in their hands and let them take him away. The last thing that they want is a problem on their hands here in Cold Creek.

The letter to the governor said:

> May 26 1865
> Dear Governor,
> This is Mayor Bruce Jacobson from Cold Creek town. I would like to let you know that there is a fugitive in our jail cell. I know that this man is wanted for murder in this state. The fugitive's name is Robert Donner. So please come and pick him up. We wll hold him here as long as you want.

The letter was addressed so they could come here without any trouble. But tonight the good mayor has his work cut out for him. But before he could send the letter he did something: he prayed. The mayor prayed that he wouldn't get killed after interviewing the dangerous fugitive. Luckily for him, they took away the gangster's gun before they took him to the jail cell.

Mayor Jacobson told everybody about what he was going to do, and everybody prayed for his safety. It's twenty minutes before nighttime. The first thing to do is to mail the letter, and the second is to get somebody to help him out, somebody brave enough to help him. That brave person is John Woody. He's around eighteen years old, six foot two, and around 162 pounds. He has black hair and blue eyes.

Nighttime came. The mayor is starting to go to the

jail cell with the backup, and that backup is carrying a gun with him. Everybody is worried to death about those two, but they're praying that they will come out of that jail cell alive. Both of them went inside the jail and closed the door behind them, and they locked it so no one would come in. The mayor told everybody that no one should come in, no matter what.

Mayor Jacobson went inside the jail cell, but John was outside the cell with his gun ready for anything that popped out, ready to defend the mayor in any way. John is hoping that nothing serious happens, because he cares about the mayor. He and his father have been good friends for more than twenty years.

The mayor began talking.

"All right, Robert, you know why you are here. Start explaining a few things for me, please."

"Listen, you. I don't care if you are the mayor or not. I'm not saying a word. I don't even care if you lock me up for the rest of my life," said Robert.

"You know, I mailed a letter to the governor of this state, and they will come and get you. You'll leave Cold Creek forever and never come back here. Most likely you'll hang for this," said Mayor Jacobson.

"I really don't care. Take me away. I don't care if I hang for this. I won't tell you where the rest of the gang is," said Robert.

"All right, it's your choice," said Mayor Jacobson.

The mayor calmly left the cell, making sure that he locked the cell so the fugitive wouldn't escape. So the mayor and John left the jail office. Everybody in Cold

Creek saw both of them leave the mail office, and they were glad that they got out alive. Everybody is glad that their prayers have been answered.

D.H. also saw them coming outside right across the street, and he was glad that they were all right. But tonight he's going to have a talk with Desert Fox. Luckily from him, Desert Fox was waiting for him right about then, so D.H. took off right away. As fast as D.H. could, he made it to the same area where he always met Desert Fox.

"Desert Fox, I would like to say thank you for your help. I don't know how to repay you for something like this," said D.H.

"You don't have to repay me in any way; just a nice thank you will be nice. What happened down at town earlier?" said Desert Fox.

"They're going to take him to another place for him to meet justice. So far, he hasn't said that much. That's all I know," said D.H.

"I can understand why. What about the mayor? Did he back off?" said Desert Fox.

"He did. He's going to leave me alone, thanks to you. I have to take off, but I wanted to come here and thank you personally," said D.H.

"You're welcome, and thank you for coming all this way," said Desert Fox.

D.H. got onto his horse and took off. D.H. did notices that something was seriously wrong with Desert Fox, but he didn't know what. Maybe, just maybe, he wanted to take on Thomas but didn't for some reason. He had his chance last wanted to take on Thomas but didn't for some reason. He had his chance last night. Maybe Desert Fox is waiting for the right time or something. D.H. spent the whole way to town thinking about this, but it was best that he mind his own business, because he wants to take him on alone, and that's it.

Meanwhile, somewhere else away from Cold Creek, Thomas is very angry about what happened last night. Most likely they are going to take Robert away, since he's wanted for murder. Thomas knows right away that this is the work of Desert Fox, and this is his way of getting even for what Thomas did to him all those years ago.

The other gangsters didn't say a word. They all knew how angry he was about this, so it was best not to say one word to save their own skin. The only thing to do right now-which is what Thomas is thinking right about now-is to find Desert Fox and all of his Indian friends before the finds him. That's what he told the guys. Since they had no choice, they did what he told them to do.

Morning came. The gangsters didn't eat their breakfast; they wanted to get an early start on finding those Indians, and they wouldn't rest until they did. Little do they know that it's going to be impossible to find them, because they are hidden so no one will ever find them. Sooner or later, the gangsters are going are hidden so no one will ever find them. Sooner or later, the gangsters are going to give up, and there is no way that Thomas is ever going to find them.

The gangsters spend all day trying to find those Indians, but they didn't find them. It was nearly impossible to find those crazy Indians. Thomas started to think that it was impossible. There aren't any Indians that live around Cold Creek. It's not like they just disappeared into thin air. That's impossible. It happen-it finally really happened. All of them decided to give up on finding those Indians-even Thomas "The Killer."

Thomas always thought to himself that nobody had ever outsmarted him, but somebody did it, and that somebody was a Indian named Desert Fox. Mark his words, he will get the last laugh or die trying, finding him and killing him once and for all. Right now, they are too far from Cold Creek, so it's best to go back before any of the Texas Rangers or somebody else takes them in, like a bounty hunter.

ELEVEN

WEEK PASSED. MAYOR Jacobson finally got a letter from the governor, and they would pick Robert Donner up right away. Everybody in town heard the good news and was glad that justice was helping each and every one of them. But by now Thomas "The Killer" has heard what happened, and he's going to get even one way or the other.

Every day for the past week, Thomas looked through Cold Creek to see when they were moving Robert so he could save him from being hung to death by the government. Thomas wanted revenge on those Indians for trying to take him and his gang on, and he knew right away that Desert Fox was getting the last laugh. But soon Thomas would get the last laugh.

It's Friday by now, and Thomas is waiting for them to

take Robert out of the jail cell. At high noon it happened, so he gang got ready. There's about ten Texas Rangers taking him to another state to face the judge for all his murders, and Thomas and the gang are ready to follow them for a good old-fashioned hung.

Ten miles north of Cold Creek, Thomas and the gang are right behind the Rangers. Then as fast as they can, Thomas and his gang are right behind them, and they don't even notices them. All of them got out their guns and started to shoot at them in cold blood, and in less than a second the Rangers were on the ground bleeding to death, but there was no one to help them at all.

"Thanks, guys. I don't know what I'll do without you guys," said Robert.

"Don't worry about it. Now let's get out of there and leave these Texas Rangers to die," said Thomas.

"All right, let's get out of here," said Robert.

Frank untied Robert and took all of the Rangers' guns for some extra bullets for any kind of showdown. Robert is glad that he's still a free man and won't have to worry about getting hanged on any rope for a very long time. Right now all of them are getting back to Cold Creek without any trouble.

Thomas sure is wishing to see on the looks on the faces of everybody in town when they see what he ahs done to save one of his gang-murdering all those innocent Texas Rangers. Sooner or later, all of them will find out and give the message to Desert Fox that he's coming after him to kill him.

Right now back at Cold Creek, everybody is safe

and sound, thinking they may go outside to have a little fun for a change. But they're not getting their hopes up knowing that Thomas "The Killer" is out here planning to do God knows what to them. It's nighttime, so everybody is sound asleep knowing that they might get up in the middle of the night with a shooting.

It's eleven o'clock at night when without any warning there's a shooting all over town and through the windows. Everybody got up, scared half to death. When al of them got near their broken windows, they got a surprise bigger than any surprise they have ever had in their life.

All of them saw Robert Donner escaped from those Texas Rangers. Most likely the gang killed each and every one of them. It was like those gangsters had no souls inside of them. Every man, woman, and child stayed low so none of them could get injured, or much worse, get killed.

Everybody saw what happened, even D.H. It's best to stay indoors for tonight, and tomorrow D.H. is going to warn Desert Fox that Thomas's gang helped Robert to escape those Texas Rangers. After a few minutes passed, all of those gangsters left Cold Creek. But they will be back for sure, and this time it's personal.

Morning came. Almost everybody got up late since there was a shooting last night. The only person that didn't sleep was D.H. After last night's shooting, nobody is crazy enough to come outside. D.H. has to wait for a message from Desert Fox to meet him tonight to tell him what happened.

Out of nowhere an arrow with a note around it came through the side of the back window, and it's from Desert Fox for sure. D.H. is really wishing that there was a easier way to get a hold of Desert Fox. The note said:

"I know about the Texas Rangers. My people have found the bodies and given them a good funeral. Me and my people are getting to the bottom of this, so you've got nothing to worry about. You are being watched around the clock, so no one will hurt you in any way. I'll keep you informed of what's going on. From Desert Fox."

The first two words that came out of D.H.'s mouth were, "Thank God." At least those Texas Rangers died proudly on their jobs, doing the right thing all the time. But he felt bad about their families. D.H. is glad that his good friend is protecting him, because he really needs some help right now. The last thing he wants in these hard times is surprises and a bullet right through him.

Nighttime came. D.H. really needs some fresh air, since he was indoors all day. He needs a walk in a good fresh air, and at the same time he's being watched by his good friend Desert Fox. Little does D.H. know that somebody is following him. But then D.H. heard something right behind him, and he turned around to see who it was.

What a surprise he had. It's Thomas "The Killer" with a gun out ready to shoot him. But D.H. isn't afraid of him or his men, who aren't around. It's just him. For a minute or two they both looked at each other but they didn't move a muscle. So far, both of them don't what to believe.

"All right, we are both alone out here. I've go this to ask you. What are you going to do? Kill me, or what?" said D.H.

"You are a brave man for coming out in the middle of the night without any worries. I like that, but I've got to ask you. Why aren't you afraid? Usually I know when somebody is afraid or not, and you're not afraid," said Thomas.

"Boy, would you like to know," said D.H.

"What is that supposed to mean?" said Thomas.

"I'm protected by the Indians around here in Cold Creek, and right about now there's a Indian across the street with a loaded gun, ready to shoot you to death if you don't leave," said D.H.

"So you must be the one that Desert Fox is getting all of the help from. I should've known that he might have some help on this," said Thomas.

"Pretty much, Thomas," said D.H.

"I'm leaving tonight. You are a very lucky rabbit that I'm not hunting you down at all. I don't know how lucky can one person can be," said Thomas.

Thomas put down his gun and took off into the night without any trace. D.H. is very lucky that he's being watched and protected by the Indians. So far, D.H. has very lucky that he has had a friend to help him out. By now the Indians left that was watching D.H. and another Indian came. But the one that left told Desert Fox, and he was glad that his good friend wasn't dead from that monster.

On the ride to the hideout, Thomas has been doing

some thinking. The best way to get through to Desert Fox is killing one of his friends or family, like he did before to get to him. The question is, where are they hiding? That's the problem. Nobody knows where those Indians are hiding out. Nobody in town knows that there are Indians around this land.

Thomas isn't worried. If he finds one, he will personally shoot one. That will get through to Desert Fox in a way he can't imagine in his head. Right now, it's getting pretty late and Thomas is really needing some rest because he had a long day. But he's hoping that tomorrow he can shoot an Indian like all could-blooded killers.

Morning came. Thomas got up pretty early to watch the sun come up. This is really strange for somebody like Thomas, but he's watching the sun coming up. So far, Thomas has a feeling that it's going to be his day for shooting on Indian to make a point to Desert Fox and everybody in Cold Creek, and even Desert Fox's friend D.H.

The rest of the men woke up a little later without any trouble. All of them saw Thomas was up, and he told them to spread out to look for any Indians. He told them to bring him here alive. He will personally hill him and take him to Cold Creek to make a point to everybody down there. Nobody said a word. They all were willing to do it, but a the same time they though to themselves that he was crazy or something. But nobody said a word.

After a few hours passed, they finally found a Indian

and kidnapped him and brought him to the area where they were hanging out. The Indian was a good friend of Desert Fox. When he saw Thomas look through him, he wasn't surprised or anything. Right away, Thomas knows that Desert Fox told him so much about him that he's willing to die for his people to help Desert Fox and D.H.

Thomas reached for his gun and pointed it at the Indian. In less than a second, without caring, Thomas shot him in cold blood, and the Indian died in less than a second. Frank and Robert picked up the Indian and put him on top of the Thomas's horse and rode all the way to Cold Creek alone. Everybody in Cold Creek will get a big surprise with what they are going to see.

They made it to Cold Creek. Thomas got everybody to notices him by shooting a few bullets, and everybody saw him through their windows. All of them were wondering what he was doing with a Indian on top of his horse, but pretty soon they were going to get an answer, and it was going to be a horrible one.

"People of Cold Creek, this is an Indian I shot in cold blood, and pretty soon I will continue killing more Indians here in Cold Creek, where you never though you would see one. The only way can stop me and my gang is to kill me, but no one will ever be brave enough to do that. SO remember, I'm here to stay," said Thomas.

Thomas dropped the Indian down from his horse and rode away as fast as he could, and everybody knew that he was serious. Thomas will kill again until somebody kills him. D.H. will have a hard time explaining what he saw to Desert Fox, but somehow he'll find out, with or without D.H. telling him what he saw a second ago.

Meanwhile, he was back at the Indian area where Desert Fox was waiting for his good friend to come back. He has been away for a long time, and Desert Fox is hoping that he's all right. It's best to go out and look for him, hoping nothing bad has happened to him. The sun is coming down and Desert Fox still hasn't seen his friend. So the best thing to do is to go out and look for him, hoping that Thomas didn't do anything bad to him.

Desert Fox looked everywhere that most of the Indians were hanging out, but not too far. But then he notices D.H. coming to the area where they usually meet. To him this is very strange but must be important. D.H. is glad to see Desert Fox. Desert Fox is wondering why D.H. is here. But from the look on D.H.'s face, it's bad news, the kind that you just don't want to hear.

"Why are you here? I didn't send for you. Something tells me you've got bad news for me," said Desert Fox.

"Yes I do. I'm so sorry, my old friend, but I thought that I was best to hear this from me before you find out from that cold-blooded animal. Thomas killed one of your people in cold blood right in front of everybody in Cold Creek. I'm so sorry," said D.H.

Desert Fox got down on both knees. This was one of those things that you just don't want to hear, but it just happened. Desert Fox is going to have a hard time explaining this to his people, that one of their own is dead. But he has no choice but to tell them. It's better than finding out the hard way.

"I need you to come with me, my old friend," said Desert Fox.

"All right, I'll come with you," said D.H.

D.H. didn't say a word all to the way to the Indian area, because he felt so bad about what had happened. Desert Fox felt like he lost his family all over again. When they made it to the area, all of the Indians were surprised to see somebody else beside their own kind. But if there was a reason why Desert Fox brought him here, they would welcome their new friend.

Desert Fox told them in his own language what had happened to one of their own, and all of them were heartbroken, feeling like they were going to die. But it was best to know then, than to find out the hard way by never seeing him again. Also, Desert Fox told them that he and his friend D.H. would take care of this and avenge his death for his people and family, no matter what. He promised them.

D.H. didn't say a word, but he understood how everybody felt about this. But he was glad that Desert Fox told him what he had said to his people also, fighting the good fight to capture that monster Thomas "The Killer." D.H. thanked him for that.

Right then D.H. returned home to let his friend go though this hard time and somehow work on this problem with Thomas "The Killer." Both of them had been through enough today, watching that poor innocent Indian die from that cold-blooded monster.

During the ride back to Cold Creek, D.H. was hoping that the one of them would get an idea of how to fight off those gangsters. When D.H. saw that poor boy died from that monster, this is personal because it will come back and hunt him in the future if he doesn't take him down. The thing was that D.H. did promise Desert Fox that he would take care of Thomas, and that was what he would do when they got him cornered for good.

TWELVE

D.H. WAS VERY proud to meet al those Indians in that area, and he was still surprised that they kept themselves secret for so many years since America was born. The main thing D.H. wants to know is how they kept secret for so many years. That's what he wants to know. And D.H. had to admit that they were nice people. He'll get that answer later, but right now he had a bigger problem in hand, and that problem is that gangster Thomas "The Killer."

Thomas could be anywhere. D.H. and Desert Fox don't know where to begin. This person really knows how to hide from the law. No wonder he hasn't been captured. There are even more problems here in Cold Creek. Everybody is scared half to death to go outside, even to check on the mail at the post office. This something that D.H. and Desert Fox have to take care of, and fast, before somebody gets killed.

That is a problem, all right. The only person crazy enough to go outside during these hard times is D.H., and that's all. Everybody is thinking that he's going to get himself killed if he does what he is always doing, and that walking outside is how he's going to get himself killed. Nobody knows that D.H. is being watched right about now by one of the Indian friends of Desert Fox. So he's safe, but he can't speak for everybody else on this. No, he can't.

The best thing to do is to go to the mayor's office and have a talk with him about what's going on. The second that D.H. got into the office of the mayor, he saw something that didn't surprise him. Mayor Jacobson was walking back and forth like he had received bad news or something much worse. D.H. was hoping that it wasn't anything serious.

"Good morning, Mayor Jacobson. I hope that I didn't come at a bad time. But I see you are in the middle of something, so I'll come back later," said D.H.

"No, it's not a bad time. Please come on it. I just need somebody I can talk to right now about what I'm going through. So please sit down," said Mayor Jacobson.

"All right, I'll sit down. Take it easy, get a deep breath, and start telling me what's wrong," said D.H.

"I suppose I could need somebody I can talk to. Do you remembered that letter I sent to the governor a week ago?" said Mayor Jacobson.

"Of course I remember. Please continue. I'm all ears.

You've got nothing to worry about. It's just between you and me," said D.H.

"Well, here goes. The governor is coming here to Cold Creek to see what happened to his men. I told them what happened, and all hell broke loose, and he's coming here," said Mayor Jacobson.

"Oh, boy. That's really a problem, all right. I don't know what to say but this, 'We're going down for this,' if you know what I mean," said D.H.

"I know what you mean, all right. I don't know how to explain this to everybody in Cold Creek," said Mayor Jacobson.

"The only thing to do is to tell the truth, because either way, they're going to find out. So I'll come clean if I were you," said D.H.

"Yeah, I guess you're right. It's best to come clean before everybody in town finds out when the governor comes here anyway. Thank you for the talk, D.H.," said Mayor Jacobson.

"You're welcome. Anytime you need somebody to talk to, you know where to find me," said D.H.

"Thanks. I'll keep that in mind," said Mayor Jacobson.

Calmly leaving the office without any worries about himself and others in Cold Creek. So right away Mayor Jacobson spread the word about the first town meeting ever in Cold Creek, and he told them was important and everybody must come. It sounds important, because he was asking for a meeting for the first time ever in the town's history.

Later on that night, almost everybody showed up in town for this meeting. Even D.H. is in the building of City Hall. There wasn't enough room in the building, so he told some of the people to go outside and try to hear him the best way they could. So far, Mayor Jacobson has never spooked so many people, but like they said, "There's a first time for everything in life." And there he goes, the mayor.

"I know what you are thinking, all of you, that it's about those gangsters. But that's the least of our worries. You won't believe who's coming here in a couple of days," said Mayor Jacobson.

"Who?" said Person 1.

"The governor himself is coming here to see what's going on down here. And we all are in hot water on this, if you know what I mean," said Mayor Jacobson.

Everybody stood still for a moment. None of them knew what to do, knowing that the governor would turn everything upside down and all hell would break loose on this. Nobody would take the pressure on this, not even the mayor, and the governor will have a hard time believing that there are Indians in these parts. All of them are backed into a corner without any help.

"What should we do?" said Person 2.

"The only thing to do is to tell the truth to the governor," said Mayor Jacobson.

"Are you crazy or something? If we tell the truth, all hell will break loose," said Person 2.

"I'll like to hear any of your ideas, guys. Come on, guys. I'm waiting," said Mayor Jacobson.

None of them said a word, because no one knew what to say. They guessed the best thing to do was to tell the truth to the governor about what was going on here in Cold Creek. They all agreed, and it was best to tell one person speak, and that one person was D.H., because he was the bravest. So D.H. stood up and decided to speak for everybody.

"Mayor Jacobson, I speak for everybody, and we've decided to the truth," said D.H.

"Thank you, everybody. I'll tell the truth, and thank you for understanding, everybody," said Mayor Jacobson.

Everybody left City Hall all worried to death about what was going to happen when the governor came here to Cold Creek. D.H., on the other hand, had to get Desert Fox to help him out so nothing bad would happen when the governor came. The last thing that he wants is somebody getting hurt, because killing a governor is a serious charge.

Luckily for him Desert Fox left him a note near the side of the window. It's tied up with an arrow, stuck to the side pretty well. The note said,

"I know about the governor coming. We will be on the lookout around Cold Creek so no one will get hurt. You've got the word of Desert Fox. Come tomorrow night to my people's land for our friend that died and give him a good funeral."

D.H. thanked his lucky stars that his good friend Desert Fox would help him out during this hard time and make sure that no one would get hurt, even the governor. So far, no one but the mayor knew when the governor was coming, but it was best to stay ready and alert. Nobody wanted to take any chances.

The next night, D.H. got dressed to go to the funeral, and calmly left the hotel without anybody knowing what he was doing. He jumped up onto to his horse and calmly too of without anybody seeing him. He made it to Indian area where everybody was waiting for him, and right away all of them got started.

A whole hour passed. This was a beautiful funeral for the poor guy that passed on. D.H. really wished that he could have met him. It was so wrong that he died at a young age. Everybody deserves to live a full life happily. Two hours passed, and the funeral ended. Everybody went to their own place, dealing with the loss of one of their own.

Meanwhile, Desert Fox went to the same place where he always goes to think about . So D.H. decided to go up and join him. D.H. could understand how hard it is to lose a loved one. So that's why he's going up to him-to talk to him ease the pain away. It's not healthy to keep everything inside, so he went to Desert Fox to talk about these things.

"How are you holding up, Desert Fox?" said D.H.

"I'm doing well. Thanks for asking. I can't believe that he's gone. He's just a child. If I only was there to help him out," said Desert Fox.

"There was nothing you could do. It wasn't your fault. Believe me, you'll get your revenge on Thomas," said D.H.

"I know, I know. But believe me, I'll get the last laugh on this. That, I promise. But thanks for coming here to have a talk with me. That helped to ease the pain a little bit," said Desert Fox.

"You are welcome. What friends are for is to help each other," said D.H.

It was almost midnight, and time for D.H. to leave. He said good-bye to everybody and said he would see them later. That also goes for Desert Fox. Desert Fox said the same thing to him and thanked him for coming here at this hard time, and D.H. took off without any trouble. He made it to his hotel room, and luckily for him, no one saw him coming in. He went right to bed.

THIRTEEN

EVERYBODY IN TOWN is getting ready for when the governor comes to their hometown of Cold Creek. They're hoping that none of those gangsters would come out and cause trouble, because that's the last thing anybody in town wants. D.H. is doing his to help everybody out in town the best way he can. And at t same time, he's being watched by the Indians so no one will outsmart him or use him in any way.

What this town really needs is a good sheriff to uphold the law and to protect this town. D.H. believe that everybody needs a hero, even a town. D.H. is hoping that one day he can be sheriff to look out after his town. And that's good old Cold Creek, because this town is part of him and now and will always be part of him.

So far, everybody knew when the governor was

coming and that was tomorrow. Luckily for D.H., he was the first to know when the governor was coming, and he informed Desert Fox. D.H. is praying that nothing bad will happen tomorrow, because the last thing that he wants is a shooting to kill the governor.

Desert Fox and D.H. knew Thomas well enough to know that would do something like this. So tomorrow Desert Fox and his people will be ready, guarding the governor secretly without anybody knowing at all.

The next day came. Everybody had the guard up, with the Indians protecting the governor. Luckily for the Indians, no one sees them, so they are safe for now. A wagon is starting to come with lots of Texas Rangers and soldiers all around the wagon, with the governor inside.

They made it safely to town without any trouble, for which D.H. was glad. Calmly, the governor came out of the wagon. The second that the governor came out, he knew right away that this town needed help for sure. First things first. He's getting down to business, going to the mayor's office to have a serious talk with him.

Everybody was wishing that they could have gone outside and met the governor, but everybody was scared half to death, even to look out through the window, knowing that those gangsters were over there. The governor has the Texas Rangers and the soldiers around him, so none of those gangsters will dare to go near him or do anything else.

There's a knock on the door, and the mayor calmly, but at the same time scared half to death, opens the door. He welcomes the governor in. The governor calmly went into the office of the mayor. He sat down, and so did Mayor Jacobson, right in front of his desk. Mayor Jacobson was scared half to death about what the governor was about to say, but he stayed relaxed the whole time.

"All right, let's get down to business. Mayor Jacobson, I came a long way to see what's going on. Now I expect you to tell me the truth," said the governor.

"All right, I understand. What do you want to know?" said Mayor Jacobson.

"I already knew that some men had been killed, and it wasn't easy for me to send all of their families letters telling them that their loved ones have been killed. There are a few things that I really don't understand about Cold Creek," said the governor.

"What is it?" said Mayor Jacobson.

"The first thing I don't understand is why there aren't any laws protecting everybody here in these town. The second thing is why Indians are around here protecting everybody here in town, and somebody else-an American," said the governor.

The governor and the mayor talked for an hour inside the mayor's office. Both of them calmly came out, smiling and shaking hands. Everybody knows right away that it went well, based on the way they are acting.

The governor got into the wagon and took off, but the mayor, on the other hand, did something. He put up a poster that said,

To the people of Cold Creek. There will be a lot

of changes here in Cold Creek, and here is one of the things. We are getting a sheriff of the mayor's choice only and there will be new laws in effect today. Also there will be new laws in effect today.

Everybody is glad. One person said to himself, "Thank the Lord." It seems like every prayer has been answered, and luckily for them there weren't any shootings today. D.H. is that something like this happened. The best thing to do was to tell Desert Fox, but luckily for him, he saw him behind the building coming down from the roof.

"All right, Desert Fox. It seems like our plan worked. Thank you for helping me out on this," said D.H.

"You're welcome. D.H. I've got to ask you this. What happened in the mayor's office?" said Desert Fox.

"It went all right. The government is going to make a lot of changes here in Cold Creek, all thanks to us," said D.H.

"That's good to hear. Change is always good in these cases, but we're not out of the woods yet," said Desert Fox.

"What do you mean?" said D.H.

"I mean that those gangsters are still out there, and you know how gangsters act. They never obey the law. So either way we're the ones that this town needs to stop them," said Desert Fox.

"That's true, all right I'll keep you informed on what's going on here with the new laws," said D.H.

Out of nowhere was shooting in the middle of the street. Desert Fox told D.H. to be careful and stay low.

He'll take care of it. D.H went somewhere to stay out of the shooting, but he was hoping at the same time that Desert Fox would be all right, and his friends that are fighting back know. Luckily, most people are inside, but not everybody made it. Some of the men are dead from the gunshots. There were six of them, but that wasn't a problem. Desert Fox and his friends took them on without any trouble, and it happened that those gangsters took off.

Desert Fox did the same thing-took also so nobody could see their faces. Everybody is glad that whoever those people were helped them out, but they can't speak for everybody else. A few of the men are dead. D.H. felt so bad about what happened with those men, but inside no one else got hurt.

Suddenly the mayor asks D.H. to come to his office. D.H. thinks that he's going to make him the sheriff of Cold Creek. D.H. is the bravest one in town and always there to look out after the ones who need help. Being sheriff is a lot of work, but D.H. is up for anything. D.H. calmly went into the mayor's office without anything to hide. He sat down on a chair, and the mayor satin front of his desk.

"There's a reason why I asked you to come here," said Mayor Jacobson.

"I hope that I'm not in trouble," said D.H.

"Oh, no, you're not in trouble. I've got an offer for you. I got to know you, and you are the bravest person that I ever knew. I would like to make you the sheriff of Cold Creek, `cause you're not afraid to look out after those who need have been meaning to ask you," said Mayor Jacobson.

"Fire away. You may ask me anything," said D.H.

"What is your real name? I know D.H. stands for something like initials or something," said Mayor Jacobson.

"It is my initials. It's short for Derek Hahn. That's my real name," said D.H.

"That could explain it. Me and everybody else in town has been wondering what that means. But don't worry. I won't tell anybody. Your secret is safe with me," said Mayor Jacobson.

"Oh, thank you so much," said D.H.

"You're welcome. I'm glad that we finally got some justice here in Cold Creek, ' cause we all really need it here in Cold Creek," said Mayor Jacobson.

"We really need it, and I'm glad that the governor came and saw how everything is," said D.H.

"Tell me about it. I'll get your badge ready in a week. Right now, I'll tell everybody that we've got a new sheriff around here, and you will get paid one hundred dollars a month," said Mayor Jacobson.

"Thank you," said D.H.

"You're welcome," said Mayor Jacobson.

D.H. left the mayor's office happy and on top of the world knowing that he was the new sheriff in town. D.H. has his work cut out for him, since he's got more responsibility in his hands. Right now, it's best to give Desert Fox an update on what's going on since D.H.

knows so much laws in his mind and abbey D.H. will go tonight since he's got nothing to do tonight.

In the early evening D.H. got onto his horse and rode all the way to the Indian area, and he saw Desert Fox and went up to him. Desert Fox is wondering what he's doing here, but he's glad that he is. Everybody welcomes him back to the area. D.H. said hi to most of the people, but mostly he needed to talk to Desert Fox.

"Hi, Desert Fox. I have some good news that you want to hear," said D.H.

"Good news. Tell me," said Desert Fox.

"I'm the new sheriff in town," said D.H.

"That's good. I'm very proud of you. This is a big honor. You can take care of everybody in town, and us," said Desert Fox.

"Yeah, I can take care of everybody, even you guys, because I care about you and your people and everybody down in Cold Creek. I thought that it's best if you hear this from me, since this a big honor for me," said D.H.

"Well, thank you so much. You want to stay for dinner tonight my friend?" said Desert Fox.

"I will thank you for inviting me," said D.H.

D.H. always enjoys hanging out with his friend Desert Fox, and he enjoyed his dinner. D.H. has never had Indian food before, but there's a first time for everything. Desert Fox is very happy for D.H., and every Indian is glad that Desert Fox made a good choice on meeting him.

FOURTEEN

RIGHT NOW AT the hideout, Thomas "The Killer" is angry about what is going on at Cold Creek and all the laws being made down there. Now Cold Creek has a new sheriff to uphold the law. This makes Thomas more angry than before. Thomas knows that D.H. is the sheriff and that he's friends with Desert Fox. Somehow he has to kill him, but the question remains, "How?" Thomas spent all night thinking this through-how to kill the sheriff and Desert Fox.

Meanwhile down at Cold Creek, the first thing to do is to put wanted posters all over town of Thomas "The Killer." The second thing is to make gallows so murderers can be hung. There are more laws that everybody knows by now, and everybody feels safe coming outside and having a good time in life. At the same time everybody is still scared going outside, knowing that those gangsters are still out there planning who knows what.

D.H. is still worried that Thomas "The Killer" is planning to kill him since he's a friend of Desert Fox, but D.H. has to be ready for anything. The Indians are still watching him so nothing bad happens, but D.H. still has to be ready. If only there was a way to find their hideout so he could easily nail him and bring him to justice.

Before nighttime came, Thomas just thought of something. He'll do a surprise attack on D.H.-one that he'll never forget a second before dies. The first thing is to follow him around to find out his schedule and where he goes. And when the time is right, he'll be gone, and he won't even know what hit him.

Little does Thomas know that D.H. is being watched around the clock, so he's going to get a big surprise. Thomas got a couple of new men so nobody has seen them. So it's going to be hard for everybody to see who's watching him, even the Indians that are watching D.H.

The problem for Thomas is to decide who is going into town with his new men. He has a total of five new men; it's going to be hard choosing one. The best person for the job is Andy. Andy is five foot ten, has black hair, is clean shaven, and is dressed like a normal human, not a gangster. Thomas calmly called Andy to come up to him, and calmly he went up to him, feeling great about his first job.

"Andy, your first job for today is to follow that sheriff

around and know his routine so we can find a good time and we can take of him. Understand?" said Thomas.

"I understand. Believe me, you've got nothing to worry about," said Andy.

"Good. Now get going," said Thomas.

Andy took off right away with no trouble at all. He calmly went right into town. Andy thought to himself that Thomas sure wasn't joking around about how everything had changed overnight. He wasn't surprised to see Thomas's face on the wanted posters all over town. Thomas will get arrested or killed less than a second after he's sets foot into the town.

Right now Andy is going to act normal so no one knows that he's working undercover for Thomas. The second thing to do is to find the sheriff so Andy can watch him like a hawk, and at the same time act normal for a week to see what activities he does every day, and right away Thomas can kill him.

Right before Andy could even set foot inside the bar, he saw the sheriff leaving the bar minding his own business. So Andy decided to follow him, and he acted very relaxed and pretended to act normal. Every day for a week, Andy watched Sheriff D.H. like a hawk and Andy took notes about where he went every day. Andy got the notes he needed and took off, but little did Andy know that he was being watched by the Indians.

The Indians have no choice but to tell D.H. that somebody has been following him, mostly likely, they thought, it's the work of Thomas "The Killer." The best time to tell D.H. is tonight when D.H. leaves his office, so no one will see them. But right now they continue watching D.H. for normal things.

Everybody is sound asleep; there isn't one sound. And D.H. calmly left his office to watch the town all night, to make sure that no one does anything wrong and to protect the people. As he was walking down the street a little bit, D.H. heard something. Most likely somebody is following him. In less than a second he turned around with a gun in his right hand pointing at Desert Fox.

Desert Fox didn't move at all, and D.H. was glad that it was him. But he could tell that he needs to talk to him. D.H. was glad that it was him, but he thought to himself that he was about to kill his good friend and that he was glad he didn't. He calmly lowered his gun and went up to him to see what Desert Fox needed.

"Looks like you've got some bad news or something, and I 'm surprised to see you here," said D.H.

"I'm also surprised, but I had to risk it. I've got some news that you need to hear. Somebody has been following you. It's one of Thomas's gang, and he's new to the gang because nobody got hurt all right. What should we do?" said Desert Fox.

"Oh, boy. I'm glad that nobody got hurt all right. What should we do?" said D.H.

"Me and a few people will follow him, and right before he can do the unthinkable, we'll take him on," said Desert Fox.

"All right, but be careful. I don't want anybody to get hurt," said D.H.

"I understand. Thank you for caring," said Desert Fox.

"You're welcome," said D.H.

Desert Fox took off without any trouble. Luckily for them, no one saw them or heard what they were planning D.H. went to his hotel room to get some rest. Andy by now had told Thomas everything about D.H.'s schedule, so tomorrow night they would do the unthinkable to the sheriff. But little did they know that D.H. and Desert Fox would have the last laugh.

Morning came. Thomas decided to let one of his men do his work, because Thomas was still a wanted man all over the country, so Andy decided to do the honors of killing the sheriff, without any worries or second thoughts.

Andy took off on his horse and easily made it to Cold Creek, but little did Andy know that he was being watched by the Indians. Right away the Indians knows that tonight is the night that their friend the sheriff is going to get killed, so they're ready for anything. The sheriff has nothing to worry about, because he knows that the Indians are watching him like a hawk.

D.H. left his office and calmly walked down the street. He knows right away that somebody is followed him because of the sound in the background. The person is Andy. Andy got out his gun and was about to shoot him, but suddenly Desert Fox was right behind him with a gun of his own pointing to Andy's back.

"Drop the gun or you're dead. D.H., come over here.

This is the person that's trying to kill you from Thomas's gang," said Desert Fox.

D.H. turned around and saw Desert Fox holding the person that was trying to kill him, and he was glad that he was alive, all thanks to Desert Fox. Both of them took the gangster to the jail cell without any trouble. The were glad that no one got hurt and a outlaw is captured.

"Thank you, Desert Fox. I'll make sure that this outlaw gets what's coming to him. I don't know how to repay you for this, my friend," said D.H.

"Don't worry about it. I just want Thomas, that's all," said Desert Fox.

"You've got it, my friend," said D.H.

"Thank you," said Desert Fox.

Right before he left the office, Desert Fox looked both ways so no one could see him and took off. D.H. was glad that nobody got hurt or anything. For sure whne morning comes and Thomas knows that one of his men didn't show up, he'll know right away that D.H. captured him.

So far, D.H. has nothing to lose, since the outlaw is behind bars, so D.H. has nothing to worry about, spreading the word that one of the gangsters is in jail, so that's what D.H. did. Everybody in town is glad that the sheriff captured one of the outlaws. So far, everybody knows that he's doing his job of upholding the law and defending the peace.

Morning came. Thomas knows right away that one of his men didn't show up all night, so most likely he has been captured by the sheriff. Thomas is more angry than before. Now he doesn't know what will happen next. Most likely the sheriff is going to hang him, and there's no way he can help him.

Down in Cold Creek, it's lucky for D.H. that he already has a gallows to hang the prisoner, all thanks to everybody in town. So tomorrow they are going to hang him for attempted murder. Most likely tomorrow everybody in town will show up for the hanging and know that justice has served them well, and they'll be glad that they have a good sheriff that's helping them.

Evening came. Everybody moved the gallows to the middle of town, so tomorrow there will be a hanging for sure. It took everybody half the night to move the gallows to the middle of town, but it was worth it. Tomorrow at high hanging tomorrow, because the sheriff doesn't want to teach them any bad habits. All of the parents agreed with the sheriff's ruling.

Half an hour before noon the next day, almost everybody showed up for the hanging. But no children were there, because it might be too much for them to take. Ten minutes before noon the sheriff took the outlaw to the gallows. The second that everybody saw the outlaw come outside, hardly anybody looked at him.

Calmly, the sheriff took him there and put the rope around his neck. D.H. started to tell the people what he had done last night. It was less than ten seconds to go until it hit high noon....down to five, four, three, two, one. And the sheriff let go the trap door, and the outlaw was hanged to death. This wasn't an easy thing for everybody to see, but they were glad about what happened to that outlaw. He got what he had coming to him.

FIFTEEN

By now, Thomas has heard about the hanging, and he's pretty angry about it. Thomas is thinking that D.H. is going to get at him one by one, but little does he know that Desert Fox is coming after him mostly. D.H. is just helping him out. So far it's starting to get to Thomas. He didn't know how much more of this he could take, but he wasn't going to leave town if it was a fight they wanted it's a fight they're going to get.

One question that Thomas is thinking is, *How to outsmart them?* So far, D.H. and those Indians teamed up to take him and his men out one by one, so he has to outsmart them somehow. For sure, Thomas isn't going to give up without a fight. Even if he has to see all of his men get killed, he won't give up.

Right now, Thomas has to think of a few plans-

something that will catch them off guard, something that they won't be ready for. It's going to take Thomas all night, but it would be worth it, trying to outsmart them one way or another, sooner or later. They wouldn't know what hit them.

D.H., on the other hand, wasn't worried about what Thomas was planning, because he was always one step ahead of him to protect everybody in Cold Creek. And the Indians are there to protect him. Desert Fox and D.H. are working together to fight off those gangsters, but Desert Fox wants to get Thomas a lot more than D.H. wants him.

Right now at the Indian area, Desert Fox is sitting down near a fire on this lovely evening, doing some thinking about how to get even with Thomas "The Killer." D.H. understand completely how Desert Fox feels about getting Thomas because of what he had done to Desert Fox. The only thing to do is to pray and see ho this turns out in the end. That's all they can do-just pray.

Meanwhile, it's morning at the hideout where those gangsters are. Thomas just thought of something that would totally surprise those two local heroes. It was lucky for Thomas that he had enough explosives to low up a town, and that's Cold Creek. SO far nobody knew that he had something like this, and he'll been meaning to use something like this for a long time.

Tonight Thomas's new men would go to Cold Creek and put all of the belongings inside the buildings so no one would see them. One problem remained: those Indians might be watching everybody in town. How to put them in without them knowing was one problem that Thomas could not solve.

It came to Thomas-it finally really came to him-that the Indians couldn't do anything when D.H. went to bed tonight. So when he did go to bed, the Indians would leave. This would be a big surprise that one one would ever forget. Tonight Thomas would put decorations all over town for tomorrow's surprise, until D.H. leaves town or he dies.

Evening came. D.H. is doing his protecting the town. So far nothing much has been happening, so D.H. decides to go to bed. It's almost eleven at night, and it's time for some rest. D.H. made it to his house and went to bed, and that was the sign for the Indians to leave. When the lights were off was a sign for those gangsters to plan to hide the dynamite.

It took those gangsters all night to put everything in place, before the crack of light came out and all of them took off. It's 8:25 in the morning, and everybody is awake without any trouble and doing their own thing. Little did everybody know that there was dynamite planted all over town getting ready to be pop it to kingdom come.

When D.H. made it to his office, he noticed a note on his desk. The note said, *"Be aware and leave town or get killed. Either way, you are gone. If not, everybody in town will get exploded to kingdom come. Signed, Thomas "The Killer.'"*

So D.H. has a big problem on his hands. He doesn't know what to do but to call Desert Fox for his help before anybody gets seriously hurt, even Desert Fox's people. He calmly goes outside waving his hands around to give the Indians a clue to come inside. It was a matter of life and death. And he went inside pretending to be without any worries.

Two people calmly came inside wearing masks so their faces didn't show. D.H. was about to say something, but then they took off their masks. D.H. was surprised but glad to see Desert Fox and one of his people. D.H. sat down with a lot of things on his mind. He doesn't know where to begin. At the same time he is scared half to death, and it's too much for him to take.

"I see that you've got a lot on your mind. Just take it easy and take a deep breath and start at the beginning," said Desert Fox.

"There's bombs all over town. I don't know where they are, but they are inside the buildings. Nobody knows but me and you. I don't want to tell everybody because I don't want anybody to get scared half to death, putting their lives in danger. That's part of it. The other part of it is, if I don't leave town or die, the whole town will get blown up," said D.H.

"It's a problem, all right. Don't worry. We will take care of it," said Desert Fox.

"Question. How are you going around town? If they wee you two Indians, they'll know that something is seriously wrong in less than a second," said D.H.

"Yeah, you do have a point. Don't worry about it; we will take care of that," said Desert Fox.

"All right, but just be careful. The last thing I want is to start havoc all over town," said D.H.

"Don't worry," said Desert Fox.

"Thank you so much," said D.H.

Desert Fox and his friend left the office with their costumes on so no one would know that there was a problem in the sheriff's hands. D.H. is still worried to death knowing those gangsters are holding everybody in town hostage without anybody knowing. The best thing to do is to keep quiet, because the last thing that D.H. wants is to cause a gnomons.

Evening came. Everybody was sound asleep. Desert Fox and all of his men looked everywhere for the bombs in town. D.H. is in his office to play it safe. So far, none of them has seen any of Thomas's gang, so they are safe for now. It took Desert Fox and his men a whole hour to clean up all of the messes that Thomas and his men's left.

Desert Fox and his men finished everything. They took all of the bombs away to somewhere safe, in case they might use them again, but only in case they really needed them. And without any trouble the Indians went to D.H.'s office. A few knocks on the door, and D.H. got scared half to death. But Desert Fox told him that it was him. Then D.H. relaxed and told him to come in.

"So what happened out there? Did you and your friends take all of the bombs out of town?" said D.H.

"Everything is all right. We took all of the bombs somewhere no one will find them. But need a plan that will catch Thomas and his me off guard," said Desert Fox.

"What kind of plan?" said D.H.

"Suppose you tell everybody that you are leaving town, but you don't and will surprise him without any trouble," said Desert Fox.

"That will work. I'm up for it," said D.H.

"Good. And don't worry. Me and my men will be ready for anything," said Desert Fox.

D.H. got his stuff ready to leave town. Thomas's men saw him leave which no one could. Cold Creek now knows that D.H. is gone for good. Little did those men know that D.H. was going around the city hiding without them knowing. So D.H. knows that he's going to give them a big surprise when they see him.

Suddenly Thomas came with his men with guns ready and they began to shoot everything in town. But then suddenly the Indians and D.H. started to shoot at them to make his point. Thomas got the biggest surprise but at the same time was angry. Then right away Thomas pulled the trigger but was surprised that nothing happened.

"Me and the Indians already undid what you did. Not get going," said D.H.

Thomas and his men have no choice but to leave before they get themselves killed. All those Indians and D.H. outnumbered them. Desert Fox wished that he could shoot Thomas right the, but he couldn't hide in front of hundreds of people and D.H. But some other time he'll do what he's going to do.

SIXTEEN

THERE'S BEEN NO shooting for the past week. Usually that should be a good sign, but it isn't at all. That's a problem for D.H. D.H. is sitting in his office taking a break, wondering about what Thomas is planning. But D.H. isn't getting his hopes up because nothing has happened for the past week.

Meanwhile up at the hideout where those gangsters are hiding out, something happened-something that those other gangsters aren't surprised by at all. Thomas "The Killer" lost his mind the hard way, knowing that those Indians and the sheriff are stopping him from taking over Cold Creek. He's pretty much going crazy, and the others don't know what to do.

The only thing that those gangsters can do, is to stay out of it unit he cools off. They have never seen him act like this before. They all know right away that D.H. and Desert Fox and the rest of those Indians are getting the last laugh because of what they have done to them. But sooner or later they're going to have the last laugh, even if they got themselves killed.

It took Thomas almost two hours to cool off. It was so serious that Thomas started to get his gun out and began shooting toward everything, so the gang decided to hide so they wouldn't get hurt. All of the gangster were glad that he cooled off, but at the same time Thomas sat down near the fire and thought about what to do next. But the other gangsters didn't say a word or bug him. The last thing that that they wanted was a bullet flying though them.

Down at Cold Creek D.H. needs to talk to Desert Fox because something is seriously up with those gangsters, since it's been so quiet for the past week almost. He thought that most likely Thomas was going crazy since he and Desert Fox opened fire on them, scaring them off. Most likely they would come back, but with something much more dangerous in mind.

In the early evening D.H. is walking down the street doing like he always does, watching the town. Little did he know that somebody was following him, but he wasn't in danger. D.H. turned around and surprisingly saw Desert Fox. So right away they went to D.H.'s office to have a talk. Luckily for them, no one had seen Desert Fox, because everybody was a little afraid of the Indians right then.

"Glad you came, Desert Fox. I need somebody to talk to," said D.H.

"The same here. I also need somebody to talk to," said Desert Fox.

"All right, it's about Thomas. He has been quiet for the past week, and I'm worried that he's planning something to get us, since at last week's shooting we scared him off," said D.H.

"Same here. I also got the feeling that my people will get hurt by those gangsters," said Desert Fox.

"You too? I'm glad that I'm not the only one that has those feelings. Do you have any information about those gangsters?" said D.H.

"A little earlier today me and some of my people heard gunshots a few miles east from where me and my people are staying. We checked it out, but it was nothing. Most likely it was Thomas and his gangsters. He's pretty angry about last week, since his gang didn't kill anybody," said Desert Fox.

"Yeah, I can understand why he needs all the help he can get, since we outnumbered him ten to one. All right, keep me informed, my friend. And be careful. I don't want anybody getting hurt, even your people," said D.H.

"I thank you for caring about my friend," said Desert Fox.

"You are welcome," said D.H.

Desert Fox calmly left the sheriff's office. Both of them are worried to death about the quietness in Cold Creek, and the absence of those gangsters. Neither of them got his hopes gangsters. That person knows that they are trying their best to fight off those gangsters, so he's not caballing, because the trusts the sheriff. But the doesn't know about the Indians.

Morning came. By now everybody in town knows about the private talk between Desert Fox and D.H., and everybody knows right away that the sheriff is doing his best to fight off those gangsters. Also, everybody in town knows about the Indians, and it never hurts to have the extra help, even if they are a different race. One problem that remained was talking to the sheriff. But everybody trusted the sheriff, so it was best not to bring this up to him.

SEVENTEEN

IT WAS THE second week that everything had been quiet and there was a reason why Thomas "The Killer" hadn't made any moves down at Cold Creek. The reason he hadn't moved down there was because he was thinking of something to get even with those Indians around the open area and the sheriff down at Cold Creek. Somehow he's going to get even or die trying.

Thomas spent all night thinking this through and came up with nothing. Then right before Thomas could got to sleep he had an idea-something that those so-called good guys would never think of. So Thomas will get his men to outsmart those defenders of the peace the hard way, without any warning.

Right then Thomas called all of his men and had private meeting on what he had just thought of. This is something that he men will enjoy. When they had their meeting, all of them agreed on what they would do, and all of them smiled and laughed their heads off. All of them loved it.

Meanwhile down at Cold Creek, D.H. is wondering what Thomas is planning wherever he's hiding out. D.H. didn't sleep all night, worrying about everybody's safety-that's how worried D.H. is. Right now at D.H.'s office, he's glad that glad that everybody is going outside with smiles on their faces. That helped him out a little bit.

It almost high noon, and D.H. was pretty hungry, so he decided to go and get something to eat. It seems that nobody is giving D.H. a hard time with him and the help with the Indians (which nobody knows). If everybody found out that the sheriff was getting help from the Indians, they wouldn't care as long as their town was safe from those gangsters. That's all that matters.

As soon as D.H. got into his office, he saw that somebody had left a note on his desk. Right away he knew that was from that gangsters Thomas. The note said, "I want to you to come to the cemetery tomorrow at high noon for a showdown. If you do not come, I will hurt somebody in town. From Thomas."

D.H. had no choice but to go so no one would get hurt, but at the same one person to take, and it might be a trap. The best thing to do was to go outside and call Desert Fox and some of his men. D.H. knows right away that they, are watching him. Desert Fox and some of his men knew that something was up, so they decided to go inside carefully, without anybody knowing.

They knocked on the door, and D.H. told them to come in. He was glad to see Desert Fox and two of his men. Desert Fox knows that something is seriously wrong by the way that D.H. is scared half to death. The best thing to do is to sit down and listen to what D.H. is about to say. It looks like bad news, all right.

"What's wrong, my good friend?" said Desert Fox.

"This is something much worse than before, Desert Fox, and I don't have much choice," said D.H.

"Well, tell me. That's why I'm here-to help," said Desert Fox.

"All right, I'll tell you. I got a message from Thomas, and he wants me to come for a showdown at the cemetery tomorrow at high noon. If I don't make it there tomorrow, he'll hurt somebody here in town. But most likely it's a trap, and all of his men will be there ready to shoot me dead," said D.H.

"That is a problem, all right. Don't worry. Go to that showdown, and we'll back you up. You've got nothing to worry about," said Desert Fox.

"All right. Thank you so much. I thought that you would be the one that could help me out, fighting off those gangsters," said D.H.

"You're welcome, D.H.," said Desert Fox.

Desert Fox and both of his men left the sheriff's office without any trouble. This time, no one overheard them, so they had nothing to worry about. D.H., on the other hand is worried to death about tomorrow. D.H. doesn't want nobody to get hurt, not even his friends the Indians.

Evening came. D.H. had finished his pothering, so he decided to go to sleep. Maybe a good night's sleep would help him out. Morning came, and D.H. hadn't slept all night because he was worried, but so far he was all right D.H. isn't sleepy, but is ready for today's showdown, for which he's getting some help from Desert Fox and his people.

Twenty minutes before high noon, D.H. got onto his horse and took off to the cemetery. Luckily for him, no saw him going to the cemetery. Five minutes before high noon, D.H. got out his gun to be ready for anything that popped out. If any of Thomas's gang came out, he'll shoot them-each and every single one of them. D.H. likes surprises, but not these kinds of surprises because he doesn't like hurting people. But sometimes if you are the sheriff, you have no choice.

This is the biggest cemetery that D.H. has ever seen, and he's hoping that nothing serious happens, because the town is a few miles away. The last thing that D.H. wants is somebody knowing that there is a gunfight nearby and all of them getting scared half to death. A minute before high noon, D.H. is ready for anything that pops out. It is lucky for D.H. that he already has a gun to any one that comes his way-all but the Indians, because they are D.H.'s friends.

Suddenly it was high noon, and six men jumped out from behind six different gravestones, out of nowhere. D.H. got out his gun and started to shoot each and every single one of those gangsters. D.H. has never done anything like this before, but like they say, "There is a first time for everything."

D.H. isn't getting his hopes up that al of Thomas's gang are dead, so the best thing to do is to search each and every single inch of the cemetery. The last thing that he wants is somebody shooting him in the back. It turns out that there isn't anybody else, so the best thing to do is to leave. But he's wondering at the same time where Desert Fox and his people are to support him on this.

Maybe, just maybe, Desert Fox thought to himself that he could do this as long as he believed in himself. Maybe that was the reason. Whatever the reason is, D.H. is glad that he took on those gangsters on all by himself without any trouble, because he did believe in himself. And he was glad to be alive when he came back to town.

Back in town, D.H. found the undertaker, Jason, and decided to go up to him and have a talk with him about the cemetery. Jason got the biggest surprise from this, but he was glad that the sheriff took care of it before they could even come to town. D.H. told Jason to clean everything up in the cemetery, and Jason was more than happy to do it, and glad that the sheriff was cleaning everything up in Cold Creek.

On the other hand, D.H. is looking for Desert Fox and hoping that he's all right, because D.H. is worried about him. It isn't like Desert Fox, leaving without telling D.H. Less than a second after D.H. stepped inside his office, he was surprised to see Desert Fox he was glad that Desert Fox was all right, but he was wondering what had happened to him.

"What happened to you earlier today?" said D.H.

"I know I should have been there for you earlier, but I knew for sure that you could handle this on your own, because I believe in you," said Desert Fox.

"I can understand why, but the next time a little warning will be nice. But thank you," said D.H.

"You are welcome, old friend," said Desert Fox.

Desert Fox calmly left the sheriff's office. But both of them are worried about Thomas, knowing that he's going crazy about what happened to his men. There's a chances that he might go to get new men to help him out, or go crazy. Either way, they will be ready for him, no matter what.

Up where Thomas is staying, he's pretty angry about what happened to his men. This time, he's firing bullets all over; it's lucky for his men that they are not around to see this. A lot of crazy men go insane, beyond any people could go through. Right now, Thomas doesn't know what to do next-whether to take them on or hire new gangsters. Either way, he's getting even.

EIGHTEEN

AFTER A WEEK has passed, everything was back to normal-kind of-but everybody wasn't getting their hopes up on this. But everybody decided to have a little party, knowing that the sheriff was doing his job, protecting his town of Cold Creek without any trouble at all. They decided to have it his Friday, since everybody was free then from all their work. But some people are afraid to come outside, knowing that those gangs will come out.

Right now, everybody is seeing the sheriff walking down the street, watching everybody. So far, everybody really respected sheriff D.H. He was the best thing that ever happened to everybody in Cold Creek. Sheriff D.H. is very proud of what he's doing here in Cold Creek, but at the same time he's wondering what's going to happen this Friday at the party, when everybody will be having fun. He knows that those gangs might do something against everybody here in town.

Just in case, Sheriff D.H. is going to bring his gun this Friday so no one will get hurt if there's any shooting that ruins this happy time. Meanwhile up where Thomas "The Killer" is hanging out, he has no gang to help him out. If there is only a way to know what those people are doing, he'll find a way to outsmart them.

The only way to do this is to go undercover, to wear a costume so no one will see what he looks. Then he could do a little shooting when they least expect it. Thomas "The Killer" will do it tonight, since it's pretty dark. No one will be crazy enough to follow him, because he is a very good sharpshooter at night.

In the early minutes of the night, Thomas "The Killer' got a very good costume. He's going to dress up like a homeless person; the only difference is that he let his beard and mustached grow. So far, no one has ever seen what he looks like when lets his beard and mustache grow. Calmly, he went into the town, and no one could even recognize him. So he is going to fit in perfectly without any trouble.

The place to go first is Cold Creek's bar. That's where most of the people are except for the children. They're too young to drink. Thomas "The Killer" has to lie about his name, and since he is so used to lying, he'll call himself Alberto for now so no one will know who he is.

Calmly, he went into the bar without any trouble.

For a second everybody looked at him, but none of them took that stranger seriously. Little did anybody know that they were about to talk to with a serious killer. But luckily for them, none of them would get hurt form all the information they were about to give to him.

Calmly, Thomas "The Killer" went up to the bar, paid for a drink, and began talking to some of the people of the town. Without any trouble, Thomas "The Killer" fit in perfectly and started to talk to the mayor. So far, Thomas "The Killer" stayed relaxed, but he was very close to trying to kill the mayor. But he stayed relaxed the whole time.

"I've never seen your around here before. I'm the mayor around here in Cold Creek," said the mayor.

"It's nice to meet you, Mayor. I'm Alberto. I'm pretty much new around here," said Thomas "The Killer."

"Same goes here. You're just in time for good times here in Cold Creek, this Friday night," said the mayor.

"What's going to happen this Friday?" said Thomas "The Killer."

"You see, Alberto, this Friday we all are going to have a party. Everybody is welcome, but a few people are a little bit afraid to come outside," said the mayor.

"I can understand why. It's not a safe world out there. You never know who you can trust now a days," said Thomas "The Killer."

"Yeah, see you this Friday night," said the mayor.

Calmly, Thomas "The Killer" left the bar without anybody knowing who he really was. So Thomas "The Killer" is going to get the last laugh on them. Without any trouble, Thomas "The Killer" left town without anybody knowing who he really was. So far he's a pretty good actor at hiding who he really is.

He made it to the hideout without any trouble. Thomas "The Killer" gave himself a shave and a bath, and he was all set for this Friday. It's only Thursday, but he'll be ready for this tomorrow. Right now, Thomas "The Killer" has to think of a way to surprise them without them expecting it.

Friday finally came. Thomas "The Killer" is happy like crazy knowing that he's gong to do something out of the normal tonight. Meanwhile down at Cold Creek, everybody is starting to get ready for tonight's event. Everybody seems to be happier than they've been in a long time. It happened-it finally really happened. Nighttime came and everybody was outside dancing and enjoying their meal, even D.H.

Up on top of the church, Thomas "The Killer" is hiding out and starting to get his gun out, all ready to shoot there is a bullet with the sheriff's name in it Thomas "The Killer" wants to give a message to everybody in town. In less then a second he began shooting at everything he could see, and everybody started to get scared and hide somewhere that they wouldn't get hurt.

Even the sheriff is hiding somewhere so he won't get hurt in any way. So far, nobody could even see the shooter or where he was coming from. Then the shooting stopped. Thomas "The Killer" jumped out of the church onto his horse and started to run away. He was laughing, knowing that he gave a powerful message to everybody.

The first thing for the sheriff to do is to make sure that everybody is all right form the shooting and that everybody is safe, for which the sheriff is glad. Right now, the sheriff is pretty angry about what happened and what that outlaw did. He own dying wish is that he'll get even for what he has done, some way, somehow.

NINETEEN

Morning came. Sheriff D.H. sleep all night because he was watching everybody in town so no other's would give any more surprises to everybody in town. One question remained: how did Thomas "The Killer" find out about the party that everybody in town was planning. It was a miracle that no one got hurt or anything. Everybody thanked their lucky stars for that.

Quietly, the mayor went to the sheriff's office, since it was daytime. SO far calmly went there without anybody knowing. The mayor had some information that the sheriff might want to know. The mayor has some blame this. There was a knock on the door, and the sheriff told the person to come in. Surprisingly he saw the mayor coming in, all depressed. It looked like there was something on his mind that he wanted to get off his back, and the mayor sat down right in front of him.

"Something tells me that you've got something to get off you back," said Sheriff D.H.

"I do. This isn't easy for me, and nobody knows about this," said the mayor.

"Tell me then," said Sheriff D.H.

"I'm the one who told that outlaw what was going on last night, but I didn't know, because he was dressed like somebody else. I'm telling you the truth," said the mayor.

"I believe you in my heart since we've been good friends for a long time. So you've got nothing to worry about. And also, what we were talking about is between you and me," said Sheriff D.H.

"Thank you, but I've got this to say. He's starting to get desperate because he came alone without any backup," said the mayor.

"I know. Since last night, everybody seems to get the picture on that," said Sheriff D.H.

"What are we going to do?" said the mayor.

"Stay low for a little bite until I get some answers. But you and everybody have got nothing to worry about. You've got my word. But keep this between you and me. Understand?" said Sheriff D.H.

"Yeah, I understand," said the mayor.

The mayor calmly left the sheriff's office without any trouble and kept everything that they talked about to himself. Not one soul would ever know. Sheriff D.H. is glad that the mayor told him what happened to get it off his chest. So the sheriff has to get to the bottom of this before anybody gets hurt. That's the last thing he wants.

Meanwhile up where Thomas "The Killer is hiding out, he's happy about what he did to those people in Cold Creek. One problem remaining in his head is how to plan his next idea to get even for what they did to him. Right now, he needs men to help him who are not afraid of killing somebody without thinking twice. So he really needs a miracle to get some men to help him out in this kind of way.

Pretty soon Thomas "The Killer" is going to get his wish. Up in a prison twenty-five miles north of Cold Creek, four of the most dangerous outlaws have escaped from prison and have decided to go south where Cold Creek is. They figure, they won't be found there, because they know that people can get away from anything down there. So there they go.

It took them all night to made it to Cold Creek. Then suddenly one of them noticed a light near the hills a few miles northeast of Cold Creek. The best thing to do is to investigate. The closer they get, the more they notice Thomas "The Killer." They're glad to see somebody on their side of the law. The best thing to do is to go and introduce themselves.

In less than a second Thomas "The Killer" heard something a little bite down the road and got out his gun and started to point it at somebody, and it's one of those gangsters that escaped from prison. Thomas was glad to see outlaws besides himself for change, so he put down his gun and asked him to with down him so they could talk a little bit. All four of them are glad that he didn't shoot them, because that's the last thing that they wanted after escaping from prison.

"My name is Frank," said Frank.

"I'm Josh," said Josh.

"I'm Robert," said Robert.

"I'm Victor," said Victor.

"You know any name already, but if you don't, I'm Thomas "The Killer," one of the most dangerous gangsters that ever walked this planet ever," said Thomas.

"They've got a sheriff down there? Oh boy, that's what we need-already another sheriff to take use back to prison" said Robert.

"We can deal with him," said Josh.

"This isn't a normal sheriff. He has backup from the Indians here in this valley, so we've got no choice but to think this through before we get our heads shot off. So stop and think," said Thomas.

"You're right. We should stop and think about this before our heads get shot off," said Victor.

"So you guys want join me. Be my guest, and think of something to outsmart that sheriff and those Indians" said Thomas.

"I speak for everybody, and we want to join you. It's a lot better than going behind bars," said Frank.

"That's more like it. Now think of something right now," said Thomas.

All of them spent all night to think of something, but sooner or later all five of them went to sleep, because they needed rest to get some energy inside of them for the next day. Little did they know that tomorrow the sheriff would find out that these four dangerous outlaws had escaped form prison.

Morning came. A person came into Cold Creek all alone. He was around six feet tall with a serious face. He came to Cold Creek without trouble. Everybody in town looked at him in a strange way, like he had something to hide. The first place that he went was to the sheriff's office.

There was a knocked on the door, and the sheriff told the person to come in. The second the person came in, the good sheriff knew that he was from the side of justice with some serious news. The person calmly sat down, and both of them got down to serious business without any jokes.

"How can I help you, sir? I'm Sheriff D.H.," said D.H.

"It's nice to meet you. I'm Lloyd William. I'm a guard from the prison twenty-five miles north of here. I have some bad news that you must hear," said Lloyd.

"Tell me," said D.H.

"Four dangerous inmate escaped from prison and they might be coming down here to raise havoc of here so I'm very worried about everybody's safety" said Lloyd.

"Oh, boy, this just what I need at this moment," said D.H.

"What do you mean?" said Lloyd.

"There's a gangsters out there that's already doing

something like that here in this town. I'm trying to find him. If those four team up with that gangster, they will do something ten times worse than before," said D.H.

"It's something, all right. Here's the pictures of what they look like. It's best to pass them around and be careful like before. We both don't want all havoc to break loose," said Lloyd.

"Tell me about it. All right, I'll pass these around," said D.H.

"Thank you," said Lloyd.

"You're welcome" said D.H.

Lloyd calmly left the office. So D.H. got a big surprise with the news he heard, knowing that those gangsters might team up and raise havoc all over Cold Creek. At least D.H. got a heads-up knowing what might happen here in this town. But he had to do something to outsmart them before somebody got hurt. So far nobody in town will take the news really well, but it's best to tell them now, or they might find out the hard way.

TWENTY

A DAY LATER, SHERIFF D.H. told everybody in town. They didn't take the news well, knowing that there were a few gangsters out there planning something to kill them. Everybody knows that the sheriff is going to be there defending them from those gangsters, but they don't know how. But the sheriff will think of something; he always does.

Right now, the sheriff is in his office wondering what to do. The only option that the sheriff has is to ask for help from his good friend Desert Fox. The best place to go is the Indian area where they are staying. It seems like the good sheriff needs some help on this. The last thing he wants is a war between a small town band some dangerous gangsters.

The best thing to do is to go to the Indian area

tonight so no one will see Desert Fox, and to pray that the good sheriff won't come across those dangerous outlaws. In the early evening, everybody is inside, but scared to death to even go to sleep, knowing that those gangsters are out there planning something to kill them. So calmly the good sheriff go onto his horse and took off to the Indian area.

The long trip finally came to an end. Luckily for the sheriff, no one saw him or even gangsters. The first person that's glad to see the good sheriff is Desert Fox, and he knows right away that there is something on the sheriff's mind, and it isn't good news.

"What's wrong? It looks like you've got bad news to give," said Desert Fox.

"I do. I'm afraid for everybody's safety-even you people, Desert Fox. A few gangsters have escaped from prison, and they are teaming up with Thomas "The Killer" and they are planning something to kill innocent people-even yours," said D.H.

"That's bad news, all right. What do you need from me?" said Desert Fox.

"If there's only a way to know their plan, we'll be ready for them," said D.H.

"Same here," said Desert Fox.

"I've got to go. The last thing I want is somebody worried about me back at Cold Creek. And if you get any information about their plan, please tell me," said D.H.

"I'll will. You've got nothing to worry about, my friends," said Desert Fox.

D.H. got onto his horse and left the Indians area,

hoping that nothing serious would happen on the trip back to Cold Creek. He made it safely back to town. Nothing serious happened to anybody, so it was safe enough to go to bed.

Meanwhile up a the hideout where those gangsters are hiding out, all of them are thinking of something to get even with the sheriff and those Indians.

"I've got an idea-something that they won't expect at all," said Robert.

"Well, what is it? Tell us," said Thomas.

"Tomorrow night around midnight, we will start shooting at and killing a few people to make our point. By now, they've heard about us," said Robert.

"Maybe, just maybe that will work. Let's do it tomorrow. Right now we need rest," said Thomas.

"All right, since it's almost midnight and we really need some rest," said Josh.

Morning came. Those gangsters got their guns out and started to ride all the way to Cold Creek without any trouble. They all stopped a mile away, and all five of them got out their guns so they could be ready for anything, and they prayed that they wouldn't get surprise from those crazy Indians. And they took off to town.

A minutes or two later, somebody saw those gangsters coming near them, and shot up n the sky to warn everybody that they had some unwanted guests coming near them. The only thing for everybody to do is to hide inside so won't get hurt or anything worse.

The gangsters made it to town. They all started to shoot at everything in town, and there were many bullets holes all over town. A few Indians started to come out of their hiding place and started to shoot at them pretty hard-enough to hurt them but nothing serious enough to kill them. But there was one problem.

That one problem was that Thomas "The Killer" ran away, leaving his men all alone, and so they were pretty angry at what he had done. Right then the sheriff come out. He also shot at them but stopped when Thomas "The Killer" ran away. The best thing to do at the moment was to take them to the jail cell. Luckily for them, they had a doctor in town to help them out, and it didn't matter whether they were outlaws or not.

The good doctor finished them up at the same time the good sheriff sent a letter to the prison twenty-five north of there. The note said, "To Lloyd Williamson. Come to Cold Creek. We've got the outlaws that broke out of jail a few days ago, so you can pick them up. Signed Sheriff D.H."

The letter was sent with somebody that the sheriff could trust. If he rode all day, he'll make it by that night with no trouble. Nighttime came, and that person made it to the prison area with no trouble at all. Lloyd Williamson read the letter, and a few of his men started to leave right away.

Morning came. Sheriff D.H. was glad to see Lloyd, and both of them started to shake hands. The sheriff took him to jail cell, and Lloyd was glad to see some old friends that were going back to prison. All four of them were dead angry at what Thomas "The Killer" had done to them, but somehow they were going to get even for what he had done.

"How did you pulled this off, capturing these outlaws?" said Lloyd.

"Let's just say I had some help on this," said Sheriff D.H.

"That's good to hear. It's always a good idea to have help, even these days," said Lloyd.

Lloyd and his men took the outlaws away from Cold Creek and made sure that they would never escape from prison, ever. That's the least of the good sheriff's worries, because Thomas "The Killer" is still out there planning to do who knows what to them and the Indians. Sheriff D.H. is glad that the Indians helped him out on this, but he promised Desert Fox that he will get Thomas "The Killer."

TWENTY ONE

TWO DAYS PASSED without a trace of the outlaw. Then suddenly Sheriff D.H. had enough of waiting for Thomas "The Killer" to make any more surprise attacks, because the good sheriff didn't to see anybody get hurt, or even worse. The problem is that no one knows where Thomas "The Killer" is hiding out since everybody in town is afraid, except for D.H. and Desert Fox. Those are the only two that aren't afraid of that gangsters.

The best thing to do is to have a serious talk between Desert Fox and D.H.; that's the only choice that D.H. has at moment. So tonight D.H. will got to the Indians area so he can have a serious talk with him. So far D.H. and Desert Fox are the two bravest men in the history of Old West. D.H. is praying that no one will get where he is going tonight, because he doesn't want anybody to get hurt, knowing that gangster is out there planning who knows what.

At nine o'clock at night, everybody was in their house. Not a soul was outside. Slowly everybody is going to sleep, because they turn off the lights of their candles. D.H. got onto his horse and right away took off to the Indian area without any trouble. He was always looking behind him to make sure that no one was following him. After a little bit, D.H. made it to the Indian area without any trouble at all. One of Desert Fox's friends noticed him and told Desert Fox that his friend was there.

Desert Fox is all the way at the end of the Indian area and he comes as soon as he can. Less than a second after he saw D.H. he knew that there was something on his mind and it was very serious. Both of them went somewhere private so no one would hear what they were going to say. Finally, they found a place that no one would hear them, a little bite away from the Indian area-like a mile or two away.

"What is it, my friend?" said Desert Fox.

"I want to get Thomas "The Killer" no matter what, and I need your help Desert Fox, and your people. The last thing I want is somebody else to get hurt by that gangster," said D.H.

"I understand perfectly. I'm also worried about my people getting hurt by that evil gangsters. Let's go and talk with my people. We will find him, no matter what," said Desert Fox.

"Thank you so much, Desert Fox," said D.H.

"You're welcome, D.H. But remember, I want to kill him personally," said Desert Fox.

"All right, let's go," said D.H.

Both of them got onto their horses, and as fast as they could they went all the way to the Indian area so they could get Desert Fox's people to help. But on the way there D.H. was doing some thinking., hoping that no one would get hurt by all this D.H. was praying about that. They made it to the Indians area with no trouble at all. They went to the center of the Indian area so they could easily talk to everybody.

At the center of the Indian area, everybody gathered to listen to what Desert Fox and D.H. were about to say, and judging from their faces, they knew it was serious-no funny business. So far, none of those Indians could speak English, so Desert Fox did most of the talking. He spoke to everybody in the whole area so they could hear.

All of the people heard what Desert Fox said, and all of them were willing to help them out in any way to find Thomas "The Killer." But none of them wants him to find out where they are hiding. Because none of them wants to take a chance on anybody getting hurt, they have to be careful, no matter. And everybody understands why and they all are willing to do it right now.

So all of them spread out all over the valleys to find that outlaw, just praying that none of them would get hurt. But all of the women and children were to stay behind, no matter what. Most of the night every Indian in the area looked for Thomas "The Killer," but they got nowhere. But right before the sun came up, one Indians found where Thomas "The Killer" were sleeping.

The best thing to was for that Indian to go back and tell Desert Fox and D.H. where he was hiding so they could take him down. Right before he could turn back, he stepped on a stick that made a sound. Thomas "The Killer" heard that and woke up. In less than a second, Thomas got up, saw the Indian, and shot him right in the back. But the Indian continued going without any trouble.

Thomas knew right away that he wouldn't survive out there in this heat, so there so was no need to leave the same area. But little did Thomas know that the Indian did survive and went back to the rest of his friends. Desert Fox and D.H. saw he was hurt, but the Indian told them where Thomas was hiding. So right away they took off to find him, and that Indian was given special care.

Both of them made it to the same area where that Indian told them that Thomas "The Killer" was hiding out, and right away they knew it was him, a few yards from them. Luckily for them, Thomas hasn't seen them-well, not just yet-so they have to think of something to outsmart him. But for sure, Desert Fox wants him.

Suddenly, D.H. went up to Thomas "The Killer" without any trouble with a gun pointing at him. Thomas "The Killer" was so surprised to see him. He never thought that anyone would ever find him, and at the last moment he thought that it was the Indian that he shot.

"I'm surprised to see you here, Sheriff. I've got to admit you are pretty brave to come here all alone. Now put down your gun. You should know by now that I'm a pretty good sharpshooter and I could kill you in less than a second. So think twice about this," said Thomas.

"Well, you've got me there, but either way, I'll take my chances, you gangster," said D.H.

"All right, it's your funeral, Sheriff," said Thomas.

In less than a second, Thomas "The Killer" pulled the trigger. But then Desert Fox got out his gun and shot Thomas "The Killer" right in the back. Thomas started to fall down, but then he shot D.H. in his right arm, but nothing serious D.H. would be all right. And in less than a second, Thomas "The Killer" was dead.

Both of them calmly went up to the dead body of Thomas "The Killer," and both of them looked at each other and smiled and laughed a little bit. The only thing to do is to bury the body so he will never hurt another soul. But first Desert Fox helped D.H. with his arm. And that was what they did all day without any trouble.

Both of them went back to everybody in Cold Creek and the Indians what had happened, and both side glad and happy that somebody like Thomas "The Killer" was finally dead and the reign of terror was all gone. Then one day on the Christmas of 1865, both sides-the Indians and everybody in Cold Creek-met for then and forever though out ages.

D.H. would always remember the year of 1865 as full of action and the year he became the sheriff of Cold Creek. He remained in Cold Creek forever to protect the innocent. This was the year that D.H. would never forget, all right-one that he treasured for a very long time. He told his children, and the story was passed down for a very long time.

THE END.